T0367647

CROSSINGS

S. J. NOEL JR.

CROSSINGS

iUniverse books may be ordered through booksellers or by contacting:

iUniverse
1663 Liberty Drive
Bloomington, IN 47403
www.iuniverse.com
1-800-Authors (1-800-288-4677)

Because of the dynamic nature of the Internet, any web addresses or links contained in this book may have changed since publication and may no longer be valid. The views expressed in this work are solely those of the author and do not necessarily reflect the views of the publisher, and the publisher hereby disclaims any responsibility for them.

Any people depicted in stock imagery provided by Thinkstock are models, and such images are being used for illustrative purposes only. Certain stock imagery © Thinkstock.

ISBN: 978-1-4917-2298-5 (sc)
ISBN: 978-1-4917-2299-2 (e)

Print information available on the last page.

iUniverse rev. date: 12/30/2016

-Nigel

Chapter 1

I will never forget the day I died.

There was no time for me to plan or to say goodbye or to complete my responsibilities or do all of the things that I wanted to do. In fact, time ceased to exist on that day.

I cannot tell you what day or year it is now for you. In this place, the measurement of time seems to have stopped or never occurred. I catch glimpses of what seems to be the past or maybe the future, but here all that is, just is. We do not look for explanations. We are not to question, as there is no answer.

There are many of us here. Some I feel a familiarity with although I am sure have never met them. Some are completely foreign to me.

It is not at all what you may envision the afterlife to be like or what you have been taught in the churches or schools of your world. It is different. It is not life, but we are living, albeit on a different plane of existence. Our existence is

1

referred to as the Service Plane. We do not know what lies beyond it or if anything does.

Galen has tried to explain to me as much as I need to know. He is my Advocate. We are all assigned an Advocate when we arrive. They work with us on the transition and monitor our activity. It is critical to the Balance.

There is so much to tell about where I am. I have been asked to write but I am not sure this will ever be read by anyone. I do not know why they have asked me to write, but here we do not question our assignments. We perform them upon request and when asked to stop, we stop.

Normally, my writing would only detail those things that are specific to my duties, but this request is unique. I have been asked to write about everything I experience. I have been asked to keep a journal of my own activities as they happen. I do not know why.

If you are reading this, you may possibly be dead. If you are not dead and you are reading this, then something is different.

In order for me to accurately describe my existence now, you must know a little about who I was in my time in your world. This is all I know; my full name was Nigel Stakes and I lived in your twenty first century. I was almost forty-two earth years of age when I died, which was considerably young by human standards. The average male of my social and economic stature was living to be in excess of seventy years. I have surmised that maybe my life was cut short. It was certainly an abrupt ending.

Galen says that there is truth to the theory that the *good* die young. We cease to exist as humans when we are needed to be non-human. In the world I live in there is no sense of age or chronology.

The events surrounding my life and my death are vague, but Galen tells me that I lived in Service and died when it was my time.

I have many questions since my arrival. Our existence requires us not to question our role in the Maker's plan, but we are allowed to explore our emotions. Advocates are there to guide us.

When I first arrived, I asked Galen about the millions of starving babies that die in deserts around the Living Plane. (That is what we call your state of existence, the Living Plane. It describes all things that have not yet crossed into the spiritual dimension of service to the Maker.) Had these souls been so coveted by the Maker that they were taken from the Earth before they could have any impact? How did they contribute to life?

He simply told me that the Maker had determined that their lives were needed to maintain the Balance; hence their stay did not need to be very long. He also reminded me that the chronological age of a human is not a true indicator of their time on the Living Plane. This is a concept I have yet to understand. I may not need to.

You must know that there is, without doubt, a sense of good and evil and life and death that balances all that *is* and all that will ever be in your world and in mine. This is an undeniable fact. There can be no sense of good without an opposing sense of what is not good. It is like your gravity. It keeps you from flying away.

If all humans were perfectly good or bad there would be no humanity. There must be both goodness and impurity. Flaws must exist in order to achieve perfection.

The very few facts I can recall from my life are all extracted from the day I died. Galen says my vague memory of my last hours is a gift that most are not allowed to have. The brief flashes of who I was and the settings around me are not customary to others of my world.

There is no emotion about it. No resentment or feeling of loss. No mystery that I feel I need to unravel. I do not remember whom I loved, if I had children or who my parents were. I do not need to. It sounds harsh and cold but we are all stripped of all that is human and all that doesn't serve the Maker when we arrive. Our job is now solely to do his will. It fulfills all of our needs.

We are all assigned a job when we arrive. My job here is as a Scribe. A Scribe is responsible for cataloguing the movement of beings between our worlds and keeping accurate records to ensure the Balance. I normally have no memory of what I have written once I stop, so I must finish each task as it is assigned.

We are also granted a name when we arrive at the Service Plane to identify us. Our full name is intended to be unique and is derived from the last identity we had on the Living Plane as well as the duration of our task. Our names can change as we are not tied to a physical being, but preserving our most recent identity gives us a sense of organization as we move between states of being. This will make little sense to you now, but I hope it becomes somewhat clearer as I continue to write.

I am called Nigel, as I was when I most recently visited the Living Plane. I also have an identifier added to my name to ensure that it is unique. I will explain this later.

Many of us have been to the Living Plane more than once and all of us have had numerous identities.

I have been instructed to write in this language that you can understand, although I may never know to whom I am writing. I write as the Maker has assigned me. Here there is no common language, yet we all understand each other.

Below would be a translation of a typical entry for a newcomer crossing into the Service Plane.

Last Identity: James
Name: James13567
Crossover: 3rd
Job: Gatherer
Advocate: Jensen12392

James, formerly a Living being is now identified as James13567. He is crossing for the third time. He will work as a Gatherer. These are the beings that accompany newcomers crossing between planes of existence. The Advocate, Jensen, will train James and report back to the Maker on his progress.

It seems almost too human. I'm told that the process we have here is not dissimilar to the vocations and industry of your world. We have Jobs. We have an order of hierarchy. We have required work and work is a constant, yet there is no concept of compensation for work. There is no material recognition. We work because we must.

Our very existence depends upon each task and assignment being completed. Work is our nutrition. It provides our Energy. It provides for all of our needs. Yet as much as we work, the entire scope of the job never ends. These jobs are individually assigned yet completely dependent on the previous and the ensuing task of the others who surround us.

We can be moved from job to job. As a Scribe my assignment is to document events without question. At the end of each workday my memory is purged of all things that do not support my role. I am not sure how long a workday is, as I have no sense of time as you do. I know it is ending when I see Galen coming over the horizon to collect my work.

I do not only catalogue the newcomers. I also catalogue those returning to Living form. As I understand it, we always exist in both forms. We are just in one state or the other. I am currently in the non-Living state, what you may consider the afterlife. But it is still life, and it always exists.

I once asked Galen if this was Heaven. He did not know.

I am not completely sure what determines which state someone is in or what the criteria are for life or death.

Ultimately, the Maker decides, but he does seek council of the Historians and the Advocates.

The Historians gather all facts of both sides of existence.

They objectively observe the activities of Humans in the Living Plane and they observe our work here in the Service Plane. They feed the information to the Maker, but only the Maker knows what characteristics are used to determine the state of being. The Maker is the final decision on all matters and on all Jobs I am told.

Historians never interact with beings. They simply observe. They are never to be detected on the Living Plane. They often disguise themselves as other creatures, such as animals or objects to prevent detection.

It is becoming apparent to me that my writing may not be allowed much longer. It is filled with information that could lead others to question things on either plane. Galen may come to tell me that I must cease this immediately and if so, this may never be read, as it will be destroyed, purged from my memory and eliminated from all time and space. I will not be punished however. There is no punishment here. There is just work.

I do not know if I have always been a Scribe. I could have been a Historian, a Gatherer or any number of other jobs. I know I was once a Living being. That is the only previous job I am aware of. Time on the Living Plane is a job, needed to maintain the Balance.

Only Advocates and Historians are allowed to know what I once was. Galen knows, but he will never tell me and I will never ask. It is not the Maker's plan. It bears no consequence on today's work and hence there is no reason for me to know.

Galen is approaching so I must pause in my writing. If he tells me to stop here, then this ends my chronicle. If allowed to be read digest it gently and find the good in it.

-Nigel

Chapter 2

Galen has instructed me to keep my chronicles going.

I will write about my latest conversation with him. Normally, as my memory is purged, I would not be able to tell you much. Each visit from Galen would be like the first visit. But since I have begun keeping this journal and have been allowed to reference it, I can tell you about my experiences since his last visit. I suddenly have a strange sense of memories that I have somehow been allowed to keep. It is unique. Galen has told me I should not tell the other Scribes. It is my gift alone as the Maker has seen fit.

Galen always comes when my shift is over. His appearance signals to me that my work for that period is completed. I then have some time to rest and observe things around me.

All of us spend a portion of our rest time observing the Crossover of beings. We can also socialize with other beings that are at rest. I will explain more about this later.

This was my conversation with Galen as it happened most recently:

"Hello Nigel" Galen said.

"Hello Galen. Is my shift over so soon?" I responded. I sometimes ask questions to try to get more information out of Galen, thinking I can trick him. Maybe he will tell me that I have been writing for three hours or three days or three hundred earth years. Then I could tell you.

"Your shift is over Nigel. Exactly when it is supposed to end" Galen smiled as he responded.

You must understand how we appear to each other. We envision our fellows based on the Energy they transmit to us. It could be from any point in their existence, usually a crucial moment in a past assignment. I see him as a tall, dark haired man. He speaks with a slight accent and wears a business suit. Based on my sparse memories, he looks to be from your twenty first century, as I was. This may not be how others see him, but this is the Energy he transmits to me today.

Galen is like the rest of us. He does not know specifically how he got here, if he will stay here or how long he has been here. He does not even know who or what he used to be. Again, a gift bestowed upon me is my memory of my identity and my last day of life. He does know that he died when he was thirty-three earth years of age. He does not know how. We are only allowed to remember what is necessary for our role and we do not question the memories we are given. We all know the exact duration of our most recent visit, or *life* as you know it, as it uniquely identifies us.

He does, however, know his purpose. Galen is an Advocate. As an Advocate, Galen's job is to oversee the activities of beings like myself as well as council us on topics crucial to our role and to the Balance. In fact, he works with Scribes, Historians, Gatherers and Takers to ensure that our tasks are completed and that we are ready for our next assignment when the time comes.

We have not spoken of Takers yet. I will save that for later.

He even monitors some Living Beings and can, at times, be asked to provide direction to them. His sole purpose is to ensure the completion of assigned tasks. When he appears you can assume your task is complete. Until you see him you must continue to work.

"How many entries did you make during this shift Nigel" Galen asked.

"I have totaled 34,679" I responded. I keep a tabulation of each Crossing.

It is important to note at this point that each of my records represents a being moving between the planes of existence. Death or Birth as you may understand it. Each is known as a Crossing and each has an important and integral purpose to the Maker. My job is to record only.

I continued, "16,789 Entries and 17,890 Exits".

You have undoubtedly associated Entries as birth and Exits as death. That would be natural for you in the Living state. For me it is the opposite. An Entry is actually a newcomer crossing into Service or *death* on Earth, as you know it. That would make Exit a return to the Living being, or *birth*.

I understand that this will bring about much conversation and possible discomfort in some religious and scientific communities. Your death is seen as final by some and celebrated as the ultimate salvation by others. A return to Living would be seen as miraculous. This is where I must ask you to remain objective. I fear the controversy this may start would implore Galen to put a stop to my writings. I will explain this later if I am allowed to continue to write, but please do not draw your own conclusions or weigh this against your limited Living knowledge. The answer will come slowly and gently, but it will come.

"That is very balanced. Thank you for your work on this task Nigel. This is a very important shift for the Maker." Galen said, pausing for a moment then continuing in a softened tone.

"Let me tell you a little about the Crossover, Nigel." His eyes grew more serious as he spoke.

"Nigel, we must always retain the Balance between Entry and Exit. Only when life and death are appropriately balanced can this be achieved. However, when the scales are tipped too much in either direction we have an imbalance. The system breaks down. The Maker is then forced to mobilize the Takers to balance it out."

So now we reach the subject of the Takers. This is a subject that I do not enjoy explaining. It must be explained nonetheless. These beings bear the task of physically maintaining the Balance between the planes of existence, or between life and death, as you know it.

Their job is to facilitate the Entry of beings from the Living Plane to the Service Plane. We do not know what the basis for the decisions is. They may not fully know. Criteria derive from the work of the Scribes like me and the Historians, who evaluate all activity here and on the Living Plane. The Takers are given a list of Living beings. From this list and the information provided by the Historians they coordinate the series of events needed to facilitate their Entry. They then allow the Gatherers to help those chosen for Crossover.

This is where the idea of "fate" begins to loom and where clergy and scholars have lived in darkness since the beginning of existence on the Living Plane. There is no way to understand it and remain hopeful unless you live in my state. This is by design. Hope is vital to the Living experience. It drives both the *good* and the *evil* sides of the Balance.

You see if a decision is made that a being must Enter the Service Plane, the Entry is accomplished by what you refer to as "death". Death to us is just a transition. It is a movement and a change in role and state of being. It is simply a job change. For you to understand it I will describe it in Living terms.

The Maker receives information needed for his decisions from the work of the Historians. He creates a list of Living beings and assigns them a Taker.

Messengers are given this list. It comes only from the Maker.

This list contains assignments something like this:

Living Identity—David Jones

Taker Assigned—Pelding16756 Entry Date—2/2/1978

This is obviously translated so you will understand. Keep in mind that your time, the date above, has no bearing on our time. February 2, 1978 for me can happen at any moment or it may have already happened.

20 BC and 2014 can happen in the same moment for me.

Once the Messengers receive the list, they seek out the Taker who is assigned. Each Taker is given his assignments. The Taker then must rely on the reports from the Historians to understand the events needed to prepare the selected being for his Entry.

For example, Historians have a list of each Being's existence. Consider it a resume of sorts. I spoke before of the Balance between good and evil. This is a very important concept. When a Taker observes someone who is well weighted on the side of good, based on their record with the Historians, there may be work still to do to prepare them for their next role. In contrast, if a human has lived a selfish or evil existence, there will be conditions set in motion to prepare them for Service. Most Living beings have manifested both good and evil in their lives. This is not a coincidence. It is all part of the plan and the work of the Takers to prepare them for service.

The Takers will introduce opportunities to these beings. It is not a test as you may think. It is not to prove faith or loyalty to the Maker. It is to prepare them for Service.

I must pause here to make one thing very clear. Clear your mind for a moment and take much heed in this statement. Loyalty to the Maker is not a choice. You may think it is, but your loyalty is always with the Maker regardless of your emotions. It just is. If you think deeply on this, you will know.

Continuing . . .

These opportunities can be difficult. The way in which the selected being handles these opportunities determines their role in the Service Plane. Opportunities can include some very difficult situations for Living beings such as disease of the human form, substantial loss, powerlessness, temptation, failure or even success.

These are just a few examples of the things that a Taker will employ to bring about the characteristics necessary to identify the right beings for the right jobs on the Service Plane.

Here is an example difficult for even a Scribe like myself to understand.

A man named John is given an opportunity in the form of the disease called Cancer as a result of the Takers. His plight is critical to the Balance, but he does not know this. John struggles mightily both materially and spiritually. He fights for his life. He fears for his family. He questions the Maker. He feels both anger and sadness.

Yet through his struggles he does everything he needs to do to ensure that those around him will survive in Living form when he is gone. John uses sound judgment and bravery in facing his perceived enemy, *death*. He never wavers in his courage towards his loved ones, but it is fear that dominates his every thought. He doesn't question however. He acts on impulse driven by fear, but he acts. His actions are loving and kind. He is ready for Service.

John is selected for a job in Service to the Maker. He has experienced the presence of love and service as an antidote for fear. He has worked and served without question.

He *dies* in your world and crosses into ours.

Entry.

It may seem cruel to you. Understand first that John was always going to be selected. There was never a test. The Takers cannot let him fail. *It is impossible to fail in faith.* He needed to accept his role and embrace his service on the Living Plane before he could cross into the Service Plane. He needed to break the Living bonds that produced fear in him and turn them into loving acts.

The Gatherers appear to escort him on his journey. A Scribe, like me, records his Crossover. He is assigned an Advocate who assists him with his transition and reports his progress to the Maker who will use this data to decide his next task.

At some time, maybe yesterday or tomorrow in your world, John will be asked to return the Living Plane. He will not remember his work here in his conscious being, but it has shaped him for his next job. Each job shapes us for our next one.

The suffering seems very cold to you of course. In his Living form, John experienced great pain and his family great suffering. It prepared him for his role here. It prepared him to work without question and to serve the Maker.

John does not remember who or where he was or how he got here. He is not as lucky as I am. It is not needed for him.

For John's story there are other stories. They all connected. Each selection and Crossover depends on those before it and after it.

John's wife will endure the suffering and loneliness of being a widow in life. She misses him. She fears for her children. She will make decisions based on either *fear* or *love*. The Historians record her actions and soon, maybe in 20BC or in 2014 your time, the Takers will put her fate in motion and the Gatherers will appear.

I will stop here. The concept above is a lot to digest and whoever is reading this has probably been aroused with some fear. Fear is not an emotion that we on the Service Plane are not truly familiar with. It has been replaced I am told. Sense of purpose drives us and this leaves no time for the emotion you know as fear.

What you have to understand about our existence is that it never ends. The fear that is felt in the Living Plane ultimately derives from an unknowing of what lies beyond the boundaries of your own finite understanding.

What happens when it ends? There is no reality of an end or a beginning.

Maybe that is why I have been asked to write. Maybe you who are reading this will begin to understand, to feel purpose, and to lose fear.

I will go to watch the Crossover now.

If I am allowed, I will write.

If I am not, it ends here.

-NIGEL

Chapter 3

I entered the observation area surrounding the Crossover and the Sentry acknowledged that I could continue to write as Galen had directed me. It is not customary for records such as the ones I am keeping to be maintained. I do not question this though. This is my task, to record without question. So I will continue to write the events as I experience them.

The Crossover area is not so much a physical place as it is an event. The event takes place almost as a vision or a dream. It is hard for you to understand. I am awake when it happens, but in a state of sub-consciousness. It allows me to direct my full attention to those who are crossing. This is important to me as a Scribe as I will later document the Entry and Exit for each. I will draw Energy from the experience that will allow me to serve my purpose.

The job of the Sentry is to grant access to newcomers as well as those exiting and returning to the Living Plane. The Sentry will also allow onlookers and will enforce rules.

The Sentry is basically a by-product of the meditative state that I and the other onlookers are in. They appear to us in a form that we hold somewhere in our subconscious. The Sentry I see appears as a twenty first century police officer which is something familiar that I hold from my last hours.

As I approach him, he peers at my writing instruments. For me they appear as relatively thick, rolled parchment and a quill pen. The Sentry curls his lips as if to indicate that he is not sure if I will be allowed to bring my writing tools. His head leans back slightly as if he is trying to hear a distant voice. There is a pause.

His lips uncurl and he motions with a single underhanded point extending from his arm to the observation area. This is my indication that I am allowed in. No words are spoken. The Sentry never speaks.

"Nigel" I hear a voice call.

It is a recognizable voice. It is not Galen. I look around and see someone from a distance.

It is Sarah.

Sarah is also a Scribe. I remember her at this moment and she remembers me but I do not know if before this moment we have ever actually met or if we had experienced each other's presence before. Memories are simply thoughts executed in the immediate moment that are placed on suppositions of the past. There is no way for us to know if that thought or memory existed in our mind prior to the moment we remember it. This is another heady concept for those on the Living Plane, but here it makes sense, as we have no sense of past or future.

"Sarah. It is good to see you" I speak. I know I like her.

"Nigel, I had heard you would be recording the Crossover. I am very impressed." She smiles as she speaks.

Another important note is that emotions, such as attraction and amusement, are felt on this plane of existence. However, the smile I experience from Sarah is not a true physical smile as you could see it, for Sarah has no physical form that you could recognize. I only see what I feel and my feelings are based on what I am allowed to feel. I feel her Energy and I imagine her as I am supposed to. I shape her from the emotions that I am allowed to feel at the moment I feel them.

There is a social order to our existence here. Remember that we are not in a physical place, so we imagine what others would look like, smell like and sound like.

In this case, I see Sarah as a young, attractive brunette female Living being with a mischievous but sincere look about her.

We have no real physical senses, but we do feel the genuine *love* that we have towards each other. It is not the love that you associate with relationships, loyalty and sexuality. It is the Energy we know as Love. Our Service towards the Maker binds us. We feel it towards all fellows. There is only one purpose here and that is to express Love through Service.

I smile back and say "Yes Sarah. They have asked me to write, on everything. They have not told me to stop yet. I am very fortunate."

"Well, you are the right one for this. You were chosen for good reasons. The Maker has a plan for you and for all of us really. I hope you do well here today." She looks down shyly.

"Thank you Sarah. I am sure the Maker's plan for you is equally magnificent." I reply.

"Nigel" she speaks as her voice becomes lower and more serious. "I am required to Exit very soon. I have been asked to return to the Living Plane." Her tone is almost melancholy.

I don't know what to say. In actuality, I may not even know Sarah, yet somehow I have been allowed not only to remember her, but also to feel emotions for her.

I feel strange.

"Well, I suppose the Maker has reasons. You will be missed here," I say. My words seem forced and uneasy and I sense coldness. As I speak the Sentry glances at me. I feel a strange sense of vulnerability and discomfort.

"Nigel, I must go now. This will be the last time we speak and I must get prepared. I Exit today." She doesn't smile this time.

"Travel safe Sarah." I extend comforting words to her, but she is gone.

I am almost certain now that Galen will come to me and tell me to stop writing. I do not think I can possibly be allowed to continue after my conversation with Sarah. The feeling I felt wasn't familiar. It has caused me to question the Maker's plan. I must talk to Galen. I must ask him why I felt this way and why I was allowed to remember Sarah. But first I must prepare for the Crossover.

-Nigel

Chapter 4

I have to put my puzzled thoughts of Sarah behind me for now. It is time to observe and record the Crossover.

Each time I watch this event it will appear to me as I am supposed to see it. I don't know where the vision will come from. It will be drawn from somewhere that I have visited or will visit. From past or future as you know it. What I see will seem familiar, yet each time feels like the first. It is always new. No Crossover experience resembles another, yet the feelings are always the same. This is by the Maker's design.

The feeling of a Crossover is indescribable to those on the Living Plane. I will do my best to embody it in terms you can understand.

Feelings of total comfort and acceptance engulf all who participate in watching. It is a celebration of the very essence of existence and the validation of eternity.

When I see a person step across the threshold to leave for their next task, I feel that I am leaving with them. I accept and embrace their fate and their circumstances as my own. This is not something that you will be familiar with in your current living state. It is only felt when one has shed their living being and crossed into Service. You will one day feel it. That is certain.

Here, each individual circumstance is intertwined. We understand the feelings of others because they are truly our feelings as well. We celebrate their Crossing because with them a piece of each of us crosses. We are one yet we bear many faces and many different jobs. Each of us is simply an Energy source in the entire cosmic puzzle of existence. As one crosses to the Living Plane, we all cross. As one arrives to the Service Plane, we all arrive.

This will not make sense. Not now. I don't know if the rest of my writings will make it clearer, but I will continue to write.

So now we get to my vision of the Crossover. For me this seems familiar. I am sure this is a place I knew on my last visit to the Living Plane, or maybe a glimpse of my next. I am standing in an underground Subway station. It is cold and damp and there are many Living beings standing on the platform, yet nobody moves.

I move in and out of the people and I even stop to look into some of their faces. They appear hurried, anxious, sad, angry, apathetic or afraid. They bear all of the signs of their time spent Living and the opportunities they are now facing as a result of the Takers. While I do not truly recognize them, they are somehow familiar.

There is the young lady in the shiny, caramel colored leather jacket. She has honey-brown skin and long braided hair cropped behind her head and held in place with something red. She is frozen to me. The look on her face is one of material struggle.

I turn and see an elderly man. His look is sad and lonely. His skin is very pale and he is very sick. He wears a suit and it falls off of him loosely. He carries nothing but a cane. The veins of his hands wrap in and out of each other and protrude with a smoky blue tint, looking as if they will break the skin.

There are many others, each showing their own signs of humanity and experience and age and time. They will all Enter today. It is a joyous occasion when the Gatherers arrive. They do not yet know but they will be immediately at peace. There is no decision. There is no pain and no sadness. They will all go to Service and be given jobs, and assigned Advocates. Many of them I will document. I will register their arrival or departure.

The train approaches the platform. I see a twinkling of orange light in the distance and it is coming closer. Round disks of soft white light blink frantically on the surface of the platform. It is silent as it arrives. There is no vibration. No breeze blows. It is completely peaceful and serene.

As the train reaches the station, I feel my own soul being splintered into a thousand pieces each represented by one of the souls on the platform about to realize the ultimate state of being.

Those arriving on the train have been chosen to Exit the Service Plane and return to your world. They will step off of the train and move back into Living form. In each of their places one from the platform, or the Living Plane, will step on. The Gatherers will choose those who will Enter and the train will take them to their new job on the Service Plane.

This is the culmination of the work of all of us on the Service Plane. It is our purpose. In the continuum of the Spirit, we perform our specific function to preserve the Balance. Each task performed by each Scribe, Advocate, Historian and Taker results in one of the beings Crossing.

Some on the platform were good in life. Some were evil. They will all Enter. There is no punishment or judgment here. There is only Service.

They will all be registered by a Scribe such as me or one of the others. They will return to the Living Plane where they will be placed where needed, in your past or in your future. You may meet one of them someday.

All of the cars on the train are full. There are twelve of them. They always arrive full. The cars appear to me as silver with a red stripe down the middle. They contain no other marking. They have small windows and through them I see many. All are standing. Some look old and some look young.

They will all return to your world in the normal manner, through your birth ritual. They will start as seedlings and grow until their Entry into the Service Plane is required. Their time will be watched and recorded by Historians. The Takers will offer them opportunities needed to prepare them and to maintain the Balance. The Gatherers will eventually come for them.

The cycle never ends.

But there is something different today.

There is a thirteenth car. I have heard of such a thing. It is used by the Takers, but only in cases of extreme unbalance. It is a broken down boxcar. It has strange markings. It has no light and no windows. I do not recognize this car and it feels unfamiliar. I don't know if the others see it.

Slowly the doors of the first twelve cars open. The Gatherers emerge from the train. There is Energy and light that surrounds them that would render them invisible to those living. To you, they are blocked out by the earthly burdens of knowledge and fear, but they are as real as you are.

You may picture them as angels, but to do so would downplay their magnificence. They have been sent by the Takers to bring those required to the Service Plane. Those called are removed from the Living Plane by your death ritual.

Death for a Living being can be brutal and cruel not only to those who die, but to those who love the being that is Entering. To us, Entering is pure love and beauty.

This can only be felt once the Crossover has happened. Once you have been selected and once you have been consumed by the Energy of the Gatherers, only then will you understand the feelings of complete acceptance, peace and love, but the price is a departure from your earthly form.

It is not understood in your state of being. It never will be. It must remain a mystery. Those who have crossed the thresholds of reality that split the planes of existence are not capable of remembering the experience. The earthly mind is not adequate to fully absorb the nature of the true Soul.

That is why I am sure my writing is temporary. For those who read this would have knowledge beyond that of human capacity.

There have been some who know of both planes. They were selected and sent for a purpose. Only the Maker can allow this. Some have lived among you and you have seen them as prophets or even gods, but they were simply performing their task, and ensuring the Balance.

A being steps out of each car. They are all smiling warm, gentle smiles. Their eyes are as clear as they will ever be. For this moment, the moment directly before Birth, is the time of absolute innocence and the last time they will know the entire comfort and security of the Maker, until the next time they Enter. The rest of their Living existence will be a journey to return to this very place, this exact moment in time.

They step off one by one, each walks to the escalator that will lead them to their Living existence and their next task. They slowly ascend. The escalator is so long that I cannot see where it ends. One by one they vanish into a grayish fog that engulfs the horizon that is formed where life and death meet.

They are born to the Living Plane.

Exit.

All of the cars are now empty. The feeling I have is one of complete joy and satisfaction. It is beyond that. It is not describable in human emotions. It is a sense of ultimate purpose and fulfillment that will never end. It is complete presence of love and complete lack of fear.

The Gatherers move slowly through the crowd of beings. They reach the old man. As they touch him gently on his hand, the years disappear from his face. He is immediately filled with the love and peace of the Maker and a sense of comfort that he has never felt before.

He understands immediately what earthly scientists, theologians and scholars have been trying to understand for millions of years. He now knows that existence does not end. It cannot. He has been called to Service and his Service is required to maintain the Balance. His Service is the greatest gift he will ever receive and the greatest gift he can ever give. He knows this with just one touch. Time and space vanish. Earthly bonds are broken. Questions disappear. He slips gently onto the train. I feel all he feels as if he is I.

He is.

One by one the Gathers collect the souls for Entry, each filling me with a sense of comfort and warmth that feeds my Energy.

On the Living Plane there is much heartache around each Entry. Each story of loss and despair has been carefully orchestrated by the Takers. Years of events, sometimes thousands of them, have been precisely orchestrated to maintain the Balance. Each death is required to allow each birth. Every Entry requires an Exit and vice versa. It is the Balance.

All of the cars are now full and the platform is empty except for one of us still standing there yet to ride the escalator to Living form.

Sarah.

She looks serene, but she is alone. No Gatherer has shown her to the escalator to facilitate her Exit. She has not risen into the horizon as the others. A strange feeling engulfs me unlike anything I am able to draw a comparison to.

She walks along the side of the train. One by one she passes each car until she reaches the thirteenth. The door opens and two figures appear. They do not look like Gatherers.

Their clothing is completely black except for a band on their upper arm. It seems to be symbol of sorts, like a disfigured cross.

Behind them, as the door is opened, I see shadows. There are hundreds of them. I hear the cries of children and the moans of the sick.

Sarah steps in. The Gatherers signal to us that the train will now leave. With a brilliant flash of light, it is gone.

This did not feel like the other Crossovers. I must not question, but I do not know why Sarah has entered car thirteen or why I would be allowed to feel this way.

I must talk to Galen.

-Nigel

Chapter 5

The journey back from the Crossover gives me time to reflect and record some of my thoughts. I am not sure what this feeling is that I have. It is unfamiliar. The moment I saw Sarah walk onto the strange boxcar, my sense of peace seemed to evaporate. It was replaced by discomfort or dissatisfaction. It made me want to question. I *still* want to question. I want to know where car thirteen goes. It does not go to the Service Plane and she did not follow the others to the Living Plane. That is all there is.

Normally, I would not question. I have seen many decisions made by the Takers. I have witnessed infants taken from the Living Plane and the horrors of war and famine. These are things that you cannot understand but that I realize are part of the Balance. I have never truly questioned the Maker's plan. I know that all pain is not real and all situations are temporary. But everything I know is based on existence either Living or Service. There is nothing else.

What is car thirteen? Could there be a plane of existence that I am unaware of? The Historians are surely recording my questions. They record every thought or impulse. Every time I expend part of my Energy I alert a Historian and the act is recorded. Right now they are making notes of my questioning. They will report this to Galen. He shall most likely council me, and I may be asked to leave my job. The job of a Scribe is to record without question and I suddenly have a frantic need to question the events I have witnessed.

I want to know why I was allowed to remember Sarah. I want to know why she was put on car thirteen. I want to know where she went. I want to know why I am allowed to remember my last day on the Living Plane.

I want to know why I am asked to write.

For now I must return to my post and wait for things to unfold.

Galen may be there waiting.

-NIGEL

Chapter 6

The Gatherers have given me my list and I must now record all of the Entries and Exits and assign names.

I spoke of *names* earlier. They are very important to our assignments here and on the Living Plane. They are an integral part of the Balance.

Name assignment on the Service Plane is performed by Scribes such as me. I assign names very simply by attaching the duration of the last Living assignment to the surname of the being Entering. For example, my name is Nigel15322. I was Nigel on the Living Plane and I died a few days before my forty-second birthday or the day of my Entry. That is 15322 days living.

There is something very important to note here so you can understand. There has never been a day when a being of the exact age and given-name Entered. It is a design of the Maker. This is why it is so important that the Gatherers choose names. They are passed to the Takers who know, before the being is ever born, what day they will Enter, or die.

This may seem troubling. When we see the name Kyle43, we know that Kyle Entered when he was only forty-three days old, as an infant. But understand that Kyle was only Kyle in that specific role as assigned ultimately by the Maker. He will have a job here. His age on the living plane is no indication of his time here or his ability to serve.

On the Service Plane there is no time, so he will remain Kyle43 until he is chosen to Exit and return to the Living Plane. He may then be assigned a new name or retain his old one, and his task, his Living destiny, will unfold for him. This could be today, tomorrow or yesterday for you. Of course, there was a reason for Kyle's short Living assignment. It served the Balance. We do not question it.

If you were to Enter today you would have a name assigned. To figure out what your name would be, you simply add your days living to your given name. For you to get this in your world you simply count the days from your birth until your death.

For example, if your name is Stephen and you Enter on January 1, 2014 and you were born on October 9, 1967 your name would be Stephen16886.

There would be no other Stephen that is your exact age dying on this day. There may be a Stephen your exact age, but not one that will Enter today. This makes your name unique.

Of course, there are many numbering systems, calendars and languages. I am writing in your native tongue using your calendar in a way that you can understand what I am writing. The numbers and names would look different to others.

Galen will arrive soon. My inquisitive thoughts have surely put an end to my journal. He will find that I am questioning the events of the Crossover and Sarah and want me to stop writing. Maybe this was some sort of test. I'm sure I have failed.

I have enjoyed writing for you and I hope to see you on either plane of existence soon.

Of course, we may not know each other, but something will be familiar.

-NIGEL

Chapter 7

I have to say that I am very surprised that Galen has allowed me to continue to write. He in fact told me that my writings served a purpose and that I must continue to journal the events of my existence until I am asked to stop.

I will begin with my conversation with Galen following the crossover.

I approach my post to see Galen waiting as expected. He normally would give me my list of assignments and probably ask me about my experience at the crossover. Galen, you see, attends all crossovers as I do, but his experience is very different from mine. I do not know how he envisions it or what he feels. He surely did not picture the scene as a twenty first century subway terminal as I did. His vision may not have even been Earthly. The only thing that I can be certain of is that Galen was present. We are all present for every crossover.

The place where I chose to do most of my writing is a grassy hillside. This is a vision chosen by me. I don't know where it comes from, but I feel peace when I am there.

There is a small tree of some sort that lends me shade. There are white, wispy clouds providing contrast against the crystal blue backdrop. Birds chirp, yet I see no birds. The grass is emerald green and forms a horizon with the sky on all sides.

Galen is standing under the tree. He appears today to have greyish hair. He is wearing an oversized wool jacket and a brownish derby on his head slightly cocked to the left. This is what I see.

"Hello Nigel" Galen says. He is cheerful. His cheerfulness catches me slightly off guard. I am expecting him to be more solemn or possibly even disappointed in me.

He is not.

"Hello Galen. I am glad to see you well today." I mean it.

"Nigel how was your experience at the crossover?" he asks, inspecting a green apple that seems to have fallen from the tree. In his face I see a twinge of mischief. He is baiting me for an answer, and having fun doing it.

"It was . . . moving, as always" I offer with an uncomfortable pause injected. I am careful not to let on about my strange encounter with Sarah, car thirteen and the feelings I had.

Galen knows my feelings, but not always my visions.

"I see. I am glad you enjoyed it." He pauses and looks at his list. Galen always has a list with him. As an advocate he takes careful notes on each of his assignees. He makes a note and I feel uncomfortable again.

"I have your assignments," he continues, completely skipping the entire subject of my strange crossover experience. I feel almost abandoned, but I quickly rationalized that his place in the Balance is to ensure the completion of tasks, and anything beyond that is in the hands of the Takers, who are surely watching me carefully now.

He hands me a list and I glance over it briefly. There are many names, more than usual. A list of Entering names has never before made me feel discomfort, but on this list I do. Immediately I glance at some of the Names of the newcomers. Angela42; just forty-two days living. Timothy27. Only twenty-seven days living. These were infants. They never had a chance. There are many more.

My perception of the fairness of the Balance seems to have slipped away and I do not know why. Where I never questioned, I now feel the need to question. Where I simply recorded, I now feel some sort of attachment to each newcomer.

These are the type of emotions that are felt on the Living Plane. They are not our reality here.

I am silent. Galen looks up slowly from his list. His eyes are cloudy and his skin looks pale.

Galen, as an advocate, feels a physical connection with all of my Energy. He is connected to me and feels my thoughts in a physical manner.

I can see that my negative thoughts are affecting him. His smile fades and his eyes darken. He begins to cough slightly and draws quick, shallow breaths.

These are human characteristics being displayed in Galen.

I have not seen this before, but I do have knowledge. An Advocate absorbs all of the negative Energy to keep it from those they represent. I can see my negative Energy is causing harm to Galen but I do not know how to make it stop.

He now starts to shake and convulse, and the more he seems to experience discomfort, the more I think of the Earthly pain of the infants and the ones who lost them, and the more I wonder where Sarah had gone.

I cannot stop the thoughts and I cannot stop the harm to Galen.

He drops to on knee and looks up at me, his eyes pleading for me to stop my damaging thoughts. Neither of us speaks.

I have to do something, so I do the only thing I know how to do. I begin to record each newcomer. I frantically record their Entry, their Job and the other details needed.

Angela42 Gatherer

Timothy27 Sentry . . . .

There are dozens more. I write as fast as I can.

The more I perform my Service, the more my thoughts return to the focused place I have always known. The questions disappear and slowly I see the lively color come back to Galen's face. His eyes clear.

My Service seems to have revived him.

It is as if I have seen him die and be reborn.

He rises to his feet, picks up his derby from the ground and places it back upon his head. I know this will be the end of my writing, and I am prepared.

In fact, based on the recent events, I would like to stop writing now.

My thoughts have actually harmed Galen. He has taken the negative Energy from me, as is his duty. If I continue with my thoughts, Galen will be overtaken by my negative Energy. His Energy will then expire and his time on the Service Plane will end.

"Nigel, thank you for your Service" he stammers, barely able to speak.

"The Maker has asked me to tell you something," he says, catching his breath.

"Yes Galen? What is it?" I ask genuinely. I am sure I will be asked to stop writing.

"You have been asked to continue to write."

-NIGEL

Chapter 8

With the direction I have received from Galen I will continue to record my experiences. I will do my best to not let my damaging thoughts return.

Per my duties, I have just recorded the newcomers as they Entered. One particular newcomer was familiar. It is the old man from the Subway station.

He is called Howard28126.

His tired look is gone but he still appears otherwise to me as I remember him. I feel his renewed Energy as I record his Entry.

Howard will be assigned to Advocate Terrence21762. Terrence is a longtime Advocate. He has been here since I arrived.

He will be assigned the job of Gatherer. This means that the Historians have recommended to the Maker that during Howard's time on the Living Plane, there were experiences that uniquely qualified him for this job. He will escort beings between planes during the Crossover event. He must have offered comfort to others in his last task.

I can see how he will be a good Gatherer. He has a kind and peaceful Energy about him. He will be able to transfer that Energy to beings at the moment they expire from the Living Plane and they will immediately feel at ease.

You may think of Howard and the other Gatherers as reapers or angels of death. In our world, they are pure peaceful Energy. They are not to be feared. They are uniquely qualified for their role based on their past experience on the Living Plane and they offer nothing but comfort to those Crossing.

Howard suffered in life but also found joy. He had experiences of both good and evil. The Takers carefully examined his Living records. But his long time on the Living Plane served the Balance. His circumstances were brought about in a time of great pain, but he served well. His pain as well as his joy was necessary.

It is not cruel. It just is.

Howard will go immediately to work. His Advocate will monitor and report his activity.

As a Gatherer, administering the Crossover requires that he develop his Energy to a supreme level. The Energy is felt by the Living and this is part of their journey. In your world, many talk of a sense of peace they feel in their last days of life, once they have accepted their Entry, or death. Only in the acceptance of death can one feel the Energy of the Gatherer, which is simply a channel of the Maker.

I feel a sense of peace and love come over me, as I continue to perform my task. Each entry builds my Energy. My Energy is what gives me the ability to block out the thoughts I was experiencing. I do not feel them anymore. I am aware of them however. Galen took the negative Energy from me. It has not returned, yet there is still a part of me that yearns to know where Sarah went. I cannot seem to stop this question from coming.

I know what I must do.

I would like to ask Howard if he would like to travel with me. I feel strongly that I need his Energy to return. Something about him suggests that he can help me. We both come from roughly the same time period in our last visit. Maybe he was allowed to keep a memory of his Living experience that can help me understand my strange thoughts.

As he walks by I look up from my notes "Hello Howard" I say to him.

"Hello Nigel" he responds, with a wise and comforting smile.

"I am glad to see you are here Howard. Welcome." I say, hoping my voice is familiar to him.

"Thank you Nigel. I am glad to be here. It is good to see you." Howard speaks as if he knows me, for he does. This does not surprise me, as knowledge is not an accomplishment or a reward for effort here. It just is.

We are all equipped with the knowledge we need when we arrive. We are able to learn along the way but the Service Plane relies on all of us understanding completely our role and how we fit.

"Howard, I have an idea," I say to him. "You and I could travel together. We are both from the same experience on the Living Plane. I remember some of the things from my last day. Do you remember anything?" I asked.

I was hopeful.

You see, if Howard were allowed to travel with me, maybe we could return to a place that could help me find the answers to my puzzling thoughts. Combined with my Energy we could experience the Living Plane and possibly find answers regarding Sarah. This may stop me from returning to my negative thoughts.

Beings from my world visit at times. This is not an Exit or birth, but a temporary visit, usually at the request of the Maker. You would call these hauntings or supernatural experiences. They are very real. We are actually there and we interact with other beings that are there, but since we are not confined to your physical world we move about freely, often in human form, between time and dimensions.

If allowed, and if it serves the Balance, we can make ourselves visible for what is merely seconds in your world. In some cases, we return to live out destiny in the body of others, to complete the balance and to fulfill the plans of the Takers.

If you search your heart you will remember a person in your Living experience who appeared at such a time that it could not be a mere coincidence. They were there at the exact moment needed, for good or for bad, but always to maintain the Balance.

In order for Howard and myself to share this vision and return to the Living Plane, we must both notify our Advocates of our intentions and they will ask the Maker. We generally cannot visit alone. Only a rare few of us, as assigned by the Maker, have the Energy to return alone, so we must travel with companions. Our combined Energy, the Energy of all of us, allows us to exist in the spiritual dimension and to maintain the Balance as the Maker desires.

"Howard, I feel I need to return. I feel your Energy and I think you would benefit from the trip as well. You could also help me." I try to explain my position. I do not know why I feel I needed to visit with Howard, but I know I do "I will notify Terrence and wait for an answer Nigel" Howard says. He does not question my motives.

I feel his Energy as he disappears into the horizon.

-NIGEL

Chapter 9

I now prepare for my visit to the Living Plane. Howard's presence is somehow critical to my journey, so I await his response.

I bear no knowledge of where I will be sent, in time and space. This seems my only possible chance to learn where Sarah has been sent. My need to know grows inside my like a tumor. It inhibits my ability to serve. I feel strangely disconnected from the Maker and even from Galen. I know he is aware, and I feel he may be displeased.

I must make one last visit to him before I depart. He will provide me with instruction.

Howard comes to visit me today. I will now write of our conversation.

I meet Howard in a place of his choosing and his vision.

I walk towards the entrance of a small wooden building that is disheveled and scarred with burns. I immediately feel that this building is from Howards past. There are no people anywhere.

I begin to walk through the door. Along the pathway are scattered remnants of many lives; clothing, pictures, children's toys, papers.

The door is open and from inside I hear music from a phonograph skipping over and over again. I do not recognize the music or the language being sung. It is unfamiliar.

Inside, I see an old man, sitting quietly at a small table near a long row of bunk beds. He wears the same tattered suit I saw on the platform at the Crossover.

Howard looks up at me.

"Nigel. Thank you for meeting me here" He says, slightly cracking a smile.

"I am glad we are meeting Howard. Is this place from your past?" I ask even though I already know. This place makes me uncomfortable.

"Yes it is Nigel. Something very bad happened here. It is something that I Entered not understanding. My Advocate tells me I will be placed here until I understand. This is where I work. It is the memory I have been left with"

He looks down at a newspaper. The writing is in a language I do not recognize. The date of the newspaper is the earth year 1945.

"Did you get permission to travel?" I ask Howard.

"Yes Nigel. I did." His head rises up slowly, as his eyes looked either past or through me.

"Nigel, the Maker is aware of your motives. The Takers sense your search for knowledge. They have warned me and given me the choice not to accompany you. Terrence has recommended against it but the Maker has allowed me to decide"

His voice trembles slightly as he looks back down and fiddles with the newspaper he is holding.

"So you have decided not to go. I understand Howard. These thoughts I have, I don't seem to be able to stop them. I feel the only way I can is to visit. I understand that you must take the recommendation of your Advocate". I rattle on trying all possible angles of rationalization.

Howard's eyes lock on mine. "Nigel, I will visit with you." He says slowly, but with conviction. "But understand one thing my friend. I visit to serve my Maker first and foremost." His tone seems almost angry. It is not familiar.

"But I too have questions that need answers Nigel" He looks around at the many pictures scattered on the floor and I can see him getting pale and sickly again, as I had first seen him at the Crossover.

"You do realize that we may get our answers, but we may never again know what they were. Our memories may not be spared this time." His words are louder now as he explains this to me.

"I do realize this Howard. I am hoping the Maker will allow me to continue to write." I state, not fully understanding my own willingness to accept this task now.

"I know Nigel. That is why I have agreed to go. If there is any chance that my memories can be documented and shared with me, I must take this opportunity. I must find my answer so I can leave this place" He looks back down as if speaking to the floor.

As he speaks my excitement grows. He has decided to visit with me. I do not know where we will meet but our Energy will combine to make the visit possible.

"The Maker has given us a unique opportunity Howard," I say with exuberance as I stand up from the table. "We will meet soon to depart."

I leave Howard alone.

-NIGEL

Chapter 10

My next step in preparation is to meet one last time with Galen. He would provide any final details or instruction. We meet at the same spot, as Galen has chosen it. I see him coming up over a hill. He looks very thin, sickly almost. His eyes are bloodshot and his skin is grayish in tone. I know that it is my spiritual unrest that causes his illness, but I also know that I cannot make him well at this point. My only hope is to find my answers and to give him peace.

"Nigel my friend" each word is a struggle for him to express "I am glad to see you."

"Galen . . . Thank you for coming" I help him to a fallen log where he can sit. I draw water from the well and I begin to wash his face. I work my way down to his feet and slowly run the water over them. I am hopeful that my act of kindness will return some of his color. But the entire time I help him my thoughts are obsessed with Sarah and the questions of her whereabouts.

"Nigel, you must know that the Maker has agreed to your visit. But I feel it is dangerous for you and for the Balance. I do not know if he is allowing this simply to make an example of you." his face tightens, as though his questioning of the Maker's motives has brought him pain.

"I tell you that you must go immediately. Your presence here is disruptive to the Balance. Your only hope is to find your answers on the Living Plane."

He trembles as he talks, and his eyes are deadly serious.

"Galen, will we ever meet again?" I ask. I know that the Maker may see Galen's work as a failure, because of me. He may be sent back to the Living Plane to grow and to learn more. In this case, we may never meet again. I may just never remember knowing him.

"Nigel, we are part of each other now. Our Energy cannot be separated. That is part of the great mystery that you wish to unravel. There is so much more that you may find, now that your eyes have been opened to both worlds. My biggest fear for you is that you will find your answers. My hope is that you will understand to no longer seek them. You will not be spared your memories this time my friend. And your Living name shall be Joshua. This is how it shall be." As his words end, he drifts off into a sleep.

I know it was time to go. I also know that I will not see Galen again. Not here and not as this being. But I know he will be with me.

-NIGEL

Chapter 11

My Visit will commence immediately. There is nothing left to decide or to do. I look into the distance and I see a dark horizon highlighted with a small with a light moving toward me. It is an orange light that seems to bounce as if it is walking.

It is the Gatherer assigned to assist me to my location in the Living Plane.

As it draws closer, I see the image of a woman carrying a small lantern. She is slight in stature and seems to be maybe forty Earth years in age. She walks with a slight limp.

"You are Nigel," her strong but sweet voice says to me as she shines the light in my direction. It is not a question.

"I am." I state. I feel my anxiety dissolving as see her.

I am called Doris. She replies. I know her somehow. Her voice is familiar.

For us, to return to life is to return to the reality of fear. The feelings I have been experiencing, the living feelings of fear and uncertainty are not possible when in perfect Service. These feelings were my indication that I must return. I have been moving further from service and closer to fear. I must know why.

Yet, the closer I draw to the woman, the less fear I feel. She comforts me. Here Energy absorbs my negativity.

I look into the Horizon behind her and a see brilliant bolt of lightning with a reddish outline. The clouds allow just enough of the flash through to illuminate the hillside for a moment.

"Nigel, it is time," She says, motioning me to come with her.

"Write how you feel at this moment," she asks me. "Record for one last time what you are feeling in the presence of the Maker. It is his wish." So I write . . .

At this moment, as I prepare to step through the boundaries of time and fall between the cracks of life and death, I will write how I feel.

It is as if all activity around me is intertwined. As if everything I have ever known or experienced, every memory, every pain and every joy has led me to this moment. All questions are erased. I feel total and complete love. The woman gives me the feeling of ultimate security and warmth. I feel as if all souls who have ever entered here are enjoying the peace and serenity of my Energy at this moment. My peace and my love is my gift to all beings on all planes of existence.

Perfection.

-JOSHUA
April 12 or 13, 1945

Somewhere in Germany.

I have never shown anyone this manuscript and I continue writing in it only to be passed on in the event of my demise.

They seem to be the writings of a madman; presumably a prisoner here who has lost his faculties but somehow has manifested into his reality a vision so inspiring and beautiful that it offers hope even in the vortex of unspeakable evil.

His words are like nothing I have ever seen nor imagined. The concepts written here are so profound and so counter to what is being taught in current religion and science that I cannot see where sharing this would serve a purpose in this place and in this time. It would arouse fear and suspicion. It is not to be shared but to be applied and learned.

My name is Joshua. The year is 1945 and I am a prisoner in what is known as a concentration camp somewhere in Europe. My mother was German and my father from Poland. Both were Jewish. They met after the first war.

We were taken from our home by the Nazis a few months ago. We had been invaded and living under German occupation for a long time. There were raids on homes. Many of our friends and family disappeared over the years. Everything we had worked for was taken. Finally, we were placed on trains and separated from each other.

I have been in this camp for many months now. I am starving and sick. I do not know how much longer I will live. I do not know where my parents are. I assume they were killed.

I will not write of the atrocities I have seen. I will not pollute these writings I have found. I am profoundly aware that what has kept me alive exists in the text of this manuscript. I do not know if Nigel writes from another time or place. But somehow, the text has provided me with hope.

I first found the scripts on the boxcar of a train on my way here. I scanned through the fifty or so pages prior and it was as if a light was turned on inside me. I now know that my existence here serves a purpose and, if I believe what is written here, that the suffering endured here places us all in a position of Service to the Maker and ensures the Balance of all that is.

I have spoken to nobody about my findings. The Germans would destroy them immediately. I keep them hidden. I am hopeful that anyone finding them feels the sense of peace that I have felt in these pages.

If you are reading this text, and you are suffering in this camp, be assured that your suffering will end. You will then arrive in most glorious fashion to the place where you will serve the Maker and all mankind.

If I find a small opening in each day to allow me to meditate, I will update these writings with my own experience. I feel compelled to keep writing now. I must. It serves the Balance.

If I am found writing or reading I will be killed, or others may be killed on my behalf.

Death here is our reality. We are all here to die. Many have accepted this and many have not. For me, I understand that it will come. It will come at the exact moment that it is supposed to. I understand now that my persecutors are not my true enemy, but part of my Energy and part of the Balance. My enemies are hatred and condemnation. I must avoid them.

Each day I see innocents slaughtered and my immediate reaction is towards rage and vengeance. But the gift of Nigel's document has allowed me to see past this in the moment, as I extinguish the flames of internal anger and fill my soul with acts of pure love.

In this camp, we all have a job. I take water to the workers in the fields. This is my job. I carry two large buckets as I have been assigned to do. Each worker receives just a few drops, barely enough to stay alive. But I have learned that those who want to live will live, because they are supposed to.

Those who read this, if they ever do, years from now, may not understand the treatment of human beings as we have been treated at the hands of the Nazis. I do not understand it. I know I must accept my fate it as it happens and I must be of complete Service in the meantime. My time will come.

I walk to the fields each day and I see the guards. They smoke and laugh as if blind to the misery around them. I have learned that the only reality is what I perceive. I do not know what exists in their hearts, so I do not judge them.

That they can be so callous and fiendish about their actions escapes me. It is as if a great evil has overtaken them and blinded them to humanity. It is as if an external force drives their actions, something more powerful than any human can possibly comprehend. They make decisions based on intolerance and cruelty, but all of their actions are based on their own fear. I cannot see inside their hearts or read their minds but I imagine that there is darkness inside them which even they cannot comprehend and that they may not fully control.

To believe what Nigel writes is to believe that their existence and their actions serve a higher purpose and ensure the Balance, yet my human faculties implore me to hate them. I must not. I must not accept hatred and vengefulness as an antidote for my own fear and I must move towards love. I must perform Service to replace my fear.

I often wonder how these men feel when they go home to face their families, especially those with children. Can any man truly accept the evil that resides inside him? Do guilt and shame torture them? Do they resent the Maker for their role in the Balance? The pain I feel for them and the ability to sympathize with even the most evil of beings is a gift I have been given by Nigel through these writings.

Most of the workers are barely alive or very sick. We are not given real clothes. When hot, the sun burns our skin and when cold, the frost cuts through our bones. There are mere layers left between the elements and our very skeletons. It is as though we are being scorched or frozen from the inside.

Most of the faces I see have lost all hope, except for a few. In some eyes I still see rage and in some complete bewilderment. There are those who smile at me when I bring the water, as if they know something. I think they do.

Today the sun is especially bright. I will embark shortly to take the water to the workers and fulfill my task. My shift will last for twenty hours. Then I will sleep for four if I am allowed. Sometimes the guards will come to the barracks to take men away in the night. I am in the working barracks so they mostly leave us alone to die on our own. We are young men who can still perform labor. It is ironic that the very buildings we erect are used to kill our brothers and sisters. Most of what is expected of us today is work though. If I do my work I will somehow make it out of here, maybe today or maybe in the future. If I die here tonight, my fate will be fulfilled, as it should be.

As Nigel writes;

"What you have to understand about our existence is that it never ends. The fear that is felt on the Living Plane ultimately derives from an unknowing of what lies beyond the boundaries of your own finite understanding. What happens when it ends? There is no reality of an end or a beginning."

With this knowledge I go about my service.

If I am killed today, this will end my writing. Please read this and tell our story here. Do not hate my captors, as hate is destruction of Love. And do not mourn my demise, for I know no end.

-JOSHUA

1945 - On week from my last entry

My shift today was especially difficult. Sixteen men from our barracks were executed for stealing food. The men had saved their bread each day by hiding it. The bread was then given to the starving to try to keep them alive. There is a sense of survival here that seems to outweigh selfish fear. I believe that these men alleviated their own fear by their Service.

When the sixteen were executed, I saw the look in their eyes. It was no longer fear. Their fear had been erased. I believe, though I cannot see, that the Gatherer stood with them while they were shot and that their souls were at peace when they died. Each of them now goes on to the Service plan according to Nigel.

The guards perform all executions in public in front of all prisoners, women and children included.

Most of the young now have the look of ghosts. Their innocence has been stolen. Their souls are flickering flames that will not take much to extinguish. I often wonder if survival may be a worse fate that execution for them.

When there is an execution, we are assigned to police the bodies and take them to the incinerator. I knew some of these men in my former life in Poland. They were good men, Fathers and businessmen. But in the end, they died in an act of service. It was their time.

These men were starving themselves to provide for others. They denied themselves of their daily bread to give it to those who suffered greatly. They are my teachers.

I wonder as I write this where they will be placed on the Service Plane. I see my friend Thomas as I pull his body out of the pit. I wonder if he will become a Scribe like Nigel or an Advocate like Galen.

I feel a connection with Nigel. I feel we are one.

It is hard to comprehend, but as I read his journal, I feel his emotion. I see things as if I have been there before. It is dreamlike.

I cannot speak of my newfound faith to my fellow prisoners and friends in the camp. They would persecute me. Some may want to kill me. Faith here is very integral to our survival. The ideas that Nigel has introduced me to through his writings are not in line with those taught at the Synagogues. But if they examined these prospects closely, I think they would find that they are not completely dissimilar and that the underlying message has been masked for years in an effort to solve an unsolvable truth; that a life of Service, acts of kindness and a feeling of can eliminate fear and drive the Balance. The disturbing part is the necessity for a counter balance and a place for evil and pain and suffering.

Many men here speak of revenge; of the British and the Americans eventually breaking the back of Hitler and the Nazis and what we would do with them given the chance. These men speak of how we would like to rip their flesh from their live bodies and impale them with their own bayonets. How we would go after their families, killing their wives and their children. How we would perform the most painful of torturous acts on them and how we would exact our revenge upon them in ways as horrific as those that they have inflicted upon us.

These thoughts drive hatred through the camp, and the most hateful men will find their vengeance. I believe that their rage will balance out the good of the sixteen who died today. It will be necessary. I mourn for them in life and I pray for them in death.

For now there will be no sleep. We will work around the clock and more of us will die. Water privileges for forty-eight hours have been revoked, so I will toil in the yards, moving stones, digging trenches, watching the death of others and possibly taking my last breath on the Living Plane.

I feel calm.

My writing may stop here.

I take strength from Galen's words and I try to understand without questioning.

"We must retain the Balance between Entry and Exit. When Good and Evil are appropriately balanced, this can be achieved. But when the scales are tipped too much in either direction, we have an imbalance. The system breaks down. The Maker is then forced to mobilize the Takers to balance it out."

-JOSHUA

Raining. 1945

Just as all hope seemed to be slipping away from me something remarkable has taken place.

Today I found a young woman, tortured, beaten and left to die. I do not think I found her as a coincidence. Just as I do not consider finding this journal, or me bearing the Living name 'Joshua', used in Nigel's return, a coincidence. The Balance is at work. I feel, in my innermost regions, that it is not her time to die. She has no name, as she cannot speak. She was in a barracks that we were policing for dead bodies.

I see the spirit of a child flickering in her eyes. I don't know if she can be helped, but I cannot leave her here to starve.

I carry her to the sewing shop. This building has been abandoned long ago as most of the women have been killed or are too sick to work. There is a guard that I pass on my way, but he does not react. He simply looks at me with a hollow gaze between drags of a cigarette.

I think he knows what I am doing but he says nothing. He turns his back. I wonder if he has made a choice for good. I will never know but maybe he and I will someday meet in another time, or on another Plane of existence.

Once inside I look for a place to hide her, my entire body shaking in panic. The floor is raised with a clearance between the rafters, enough to put her underneath. She doesn't move. Even her eyes are sedentary.

I pry the floorboard up quietly and place her beneath. She may be safe here.

I tell her I will return later with water and bread and that she must not move or talk.

As I walk away, I see the guard. He glances at me, lowers his head and looks away. I do not think he will go after her. I still think Good can live in the soul of every man, as can evil.

-JOSHUA

1945 A few days since my last Entry.

I hid the book in the usual spot. The guards have not searched our barracks for some time. I think the smell and the disease keeps them away. They themselves look like specters. This misery has robbed the soul from everyone in the camp. I think, even in their minds, the guards wish this would end one way or another. Some I feel kill us faster out of mercy.

The normal forty-eight-hour punishment shift lasted an extra two hours. Fifty hours of work with no water. Many of those hours were spent in the yards, working. Most men passed out from exhaustion of dehydration. At least five men died. Others may die later. Four others were shot for trying to run to the water supply.

In a cruel means of punishment, buckets of water were kept on the perimeter of the work site. We are not allowed to go near them. Two men were chosen to carry water to the guards.

The cruelty has become common. I often feel immune to it. I try to retain my tolerant outlook, my willingness to forgive, but I cannot today. Today I want them to suffer. I want their children to suffer. I would kill them with my hands if I could. The words of Nigel and Galen make no sense to me now. These writings do not seem to fit into my world. I wonder if they could have possibly ever seen something so heartless and cold in their time.

I wonder how they can justify this as a necessary action of the Takers in order to maintain the balance.

I look for my answers in the text of these pages but today, I see only red. I feel only anger, and pain and sadness.

-JOSHUA

1945. Possibly 2 days since my last entry.

More men around me die in the night as we sleep. More men are taken from the barracks. It is too much to bear. I wonder if I will be taken next. I continue to write because it reminds me of my humanity. I hope that someday my writings will be seen.

I have been able to sneak water in to the barracks to the young girl and she has not been found. But she is still very weak. The water is from a runoff of sewage, but it is the only we have.

Some will risk disease to allow one more day of life. The human compulsion to embrace their Living form never ceases to amaze me. We will go to great lengths to stay alive, as if we are afraid to leave this plane. If we only knew of what I now know through Nigel's vision, we would not cling to life out of fear, but rather out of service to the

Maker. Accepting death would be easier, and hate and vengeance would slowly evaporate.

I have survived in this hell for many months by acts of service towards others. It has given me strength to replace fear and I know that this is my purpose. I will not stop.

Until they kill me I will continue to help my fellows in this camp.

I have decided to call the girl "Sarah", after the friend of Nigel's who he met at the Crossover. Her appearance seems to affect me in much of the way Sarah's appearance affects Nigel. I feel we have met before, but I do not know her. She is barely recognizable, yet somehow we are joined. Her lifeless stares towards me still possess a flicker of her Energy, which gives me hope.

I ponder Nigel's vision of an altruistic world where the facts of reality and the balance of good and evil are achieved through service to others. This thought gives my existence meaning.

I will continue to visit Sarah in hopes that I can keep her alive until good triumphs over evil or until our fate is realized.

-JOSHUA

Sometime in 1945. Many days since my last entry.

It is warmer outside

I must write quickly. I hear commotion outside. One of the German SS guards is screaming something.

"WELCHER VON IHNEN Schweine Wasser stahlen"

"Which of you pigs stole water."

I have been caught. Another prisoner in exchange for their life or the life of their family must have turned me in.

I am frozen with fear but my first thought is of Sarah. I pray that someone finds her and keeps her alive. Her survival ensures the balance. I know this now.

I hear shots outside. They are executing more people. I hear screams and cries.

I will be tortured and executed in public if I admit I stole for the girl. They will also kill more of us. For each thief twenty are killed.

But they will kill one hundred if I do not admit it.

I must admit what I have done, but I will tell them I stole it for myself. I must not give up the hidden girl. She is our hope.

I will save eighty lives for today if I admit what I have done. I am sad, but not afraid. I know that I am being taken from the Living Plane. I know that the guards will kill me today, and that I will feel great pain.

It is time for me to Enter.

I think not of my own pain, but of what will happen to Sarah if I am gone. My thoughts are of service. I am ready.

I fully comprehend that as soon as the bullet ends my existence on this plane, that the Gatherers will be by my side and I will know peace as I have never known before. I understand that someday this whole nightmare will be over. I may even meet some of my captors on another Plane or in another time. I wonder if I will remember any of this. Will I be allowed to remember as Nigel was? What will be my job and my purpose? I will be Joshua7361.

I stumble from my bunk towards the door. I am still writing frantically. But now the guards are coming. I must put my writings away for now. I somehow feel like this may be the last time I write.

I hope someone else finds this.

If I live another day I will continue to write. If you find this, know that I do not resent those who killed me. I have forgiven them already and I am serving the Maker somewhere.

I feel peace.

-HOWARD

April 29, 1945

I could have never imagined anything like what I am witnessing. Not even in this war. I cannot adequately describe the inhumanity.

I was assigned to a detail to liberate what are being called Concentration camps around Eastern Europe somewhere. I had heard of these, but I wasn't sure I believed it. Back in the US, there were many rumors of the extermination of the Jews and others by the Nazis, but nothing could have prepared me for what I have encountered.

My name is Private First Class Howard Mills of the 45th Thunderbird Division.

As we began to look for survivors I found this journal stuffed between the wallboards of one of the barracks. It is hard to make out some of the writing, but it seems to be some sort of religious manuscript in the form of a journal. It looks to have been written by more than one prisoner, one calling himself Nigel, who seemed to be warped in the mind, and one called Joshua.

As I scanned through Joshua's entries my heart sank. The cruelty at the hands of the Germans is unimaginable. But his service to his fellow prisoners, up until the moment of his death, has given me hope in the midst of hell on earth.

We are told that Hitler gave the order to exterminate all Jews as well as others whom he deemed impure. I imagine all prisoners that Joshua knew and helped were killed. There are very few survivors here.

Those we find alive can barely speak. Most are extremely sick and many more will die. We cannot save them. It seems the only purpose in this place was to die.

Some of those who talk have told me of giant rooms full of vents where poison gas was used to kill the prisoners. When the bodies were too numerous to dispose of, ovens were built and the people were burned, often alive.

I cannot write more today. Cold blackness has overwhelmed me and I feel desperately lost. I am having thoughts of suicide and homicide. They are real. I have not told anyone. I try to find hope but uncovering hundreds, maybe thousands of dead bodies has left me with little emotion.

I feel anger, fear and sadness.

I read Joshua's words "Do not hate my captors."

I do.

-HOWARD

April 30, 1945

Tonight I was told that we executed the German guards who were captured. One man, Timmons, told me that they stared blankly into his eyes as he killed them. He claims it was if their souls had been removed. There was no fear. No fight. I heard shots and screams, but I stayed away. I know that hate will destroy me. But tonight I hate all of this, and I hate being alive to see it.

If someone reads this, do not judge me for taking my own life. I feel that this world is no longer a place where forgiveness and mercy can live. This war has turned me into the same type of man as those guards, a man without a soul. I have no fear of death, because it brings with it an end to suffering. I do not know nor care what lies beyond my existence.

Faith eludes me.

I do think of Joshua, who died for giving water to those who needed it for one more breath of life. I wonder if the broken girl, Sarah, has survived. It seems impossibility.

If I decide to live through the night I will keep this book, and I will find anyone surviving in Joshua's family to let them know what he did. I will continue to write so he and the others buried here in these ashes are not forgotten.

My existence seems to have little meaning in this place. The war, my actions, they all seem to have been for nothing. I no longer care to love or to hate.

If I choose to die tonight it was not out of cowardice but out of apathy.

-HOWARD

May 2, 1945

It has been a few days since I have written. I have been through this journal dozens of times. The first chapters seem incoherent, as if the author, Nigel, had crossed over the edge of reality to a realm insanity brought about by limitless cruelty no doubt. Yet his message is so beautiful and positive and seems trapped in time as if he is speaking from my own past but aware of my future.

I now yearn to know the feelings that Nigel wrote about in his experience at the Crossover and the movement of spirits from one life to the next. His vision of the end and the beginning of life entrenches my thoughts.

Joshua used Nigel's words as his code for living in love and service until his final breath and along the way served many. We may never know how many he brought comfort to. The very few survivors have been transported out of the country where they will be cared for. Many may not survive long.

I wonder now if the words of Nigel could be true. I truly question another plane of existence to which we will all be called. Could there be a deterministic Balance that drives good and evil and pre-determines all reality? It seems counter to ideas of free will, fate and even religion, but it is so pure.

I even wonder whether Nigel and Joshua could have been the same man. It seems entirely probable. In the early chapters, the one called Galen told Nigel his name would be Joshua upon his return to the Living Plane. Is it possible that Nigel or Joshua simply created the other in these pages in order to avoid his stark and horrifying reality?

I think of the girl, Sarah. I wonder if she died alone. I hope she was at peace. I feel Joshua offered he comfort even in his final hours.

I am still alive. I did not choose to end my life. My death would only serve the evil that engulfs this place. The words of Joshua stuck with me as I tried to pull the trigger with my rifle to my chin.

"I fully comprehend that as soon as the bullet ends my existence on this plane, that the Gatherers will be by my side and I will know peace as I have never known before. And that someday this whole nightmare will be over."

It was not my time. Joshua didn't choose his end. He chose to serve.

As I continue to read through Joshua's writings I feel utterly compelled to look for the girl he called Sarah. If nothing else I must know she existed. I must see her. His prayers inspire me and his insistence that her life ensures the Balance compels me. It is a feeling that I am not familiar with.

I believe it is Faith.

So I am still here, and I am still writing.

-HOWARD

May 3, 1945

Today we are searching all of the barracks. We have been gathering anything we can find to help us identify victims. It seems futile as most families were completely wiped out. Entire generations are lost forever.

In one building we found over seven hundred decomposing corpses, many of them children. I have not slept much since seeing this. Another sight that has been especially troubling to me is shoes and clothing in piles, filling entire rooms. I cannot comprehend this type of cruelty, even as a man who has killed another human being in this war.

The days have been long and each ends with another pile of unknown bodies destined for an anonymous unmarked mass grave at the end of the camp. To identify the dead is impossible. We simply place them in large craters created by bombs we had dropped, and burn the bodies to eradicate the various forms of disease that have engulfed them.

With each passing hour I feel a sense of disloyalty to my own conscience. I feel as if I am becoming immune to the sight, smell and feel of intolerable evil. It can drive a person mad to see such a thing.

I am beginning to lose hope that Sarah will be found, or that she even existed. I must rest and try to make through one more day on the now fading hope of finding her.

I feel numb.

-HOWARD

May 5, 1945

Something has happened.

Two days ago we were policing one of the abandoned buildings that looked like some sort of a factory. There were tables and chairs setup in rows, very close to each other.

As we surveyed the area, which seemed to be void of any bodies, I heard a faint scratching noise. Stan Levitt was with me patrolling the detail. Levitt was a second generation Polish Jew. I often thought how hard this must be for him. He may have had family buried here in the ashes. But he never spoke of it. He simply went about his duty on a daily basis, pulling out the starved and battered bodies of his ancestry and placing them gently in the mass fire pits we had assembled.

Also with us was George Timmons. George was a goliath of a man. He rarely spoke but was a fierce combat soldier. It was rumored that, on the day we showed up at the camp, he had taken three surviving German guards and beaten them to death with the butt of his service revolver.

The other rumor that circulated about Timmons was that he had been convicted of violent crimes as a civilian and offered a sentence of life in prison, or amnesty to take part in the Normandy invasion. He had landed on the beach and survived to kill many Germans.

As we moved closer to the scratching I saw Levitt put his finger over his lips as if to tell Timmons and myself to be quiet. He slowly pulled a long blade from a holster he kept around his leg and held it at half arms distance. Maybe he was thinking a German guard was hiding somewhere. I did not think Levitt would kill the guard even in light of his heritage and personal stake in this hell on earth.

Timmons put his hand inside his flight jacket and clutched his revolver slightly. I stood behind both of them as the noise became louder the closer we came.

It was coming from under the floor.

As Levitt stepped forward the scratching became a knocking. He looked down and jumped back a few feet. Then I saw him stow his blade back in its sheath. Timmons moved his hand off of his revolver and moved with urgency to the noise ushering Levitt out of the way with his massive arm.

He reached down to the floorboard that was slightly raised from the others and pulled it up. He face suddenly fell. I didn't yet have a look at what he was staring at. I saw Levitt turn and look away.

I moved closer, not sure I wanted to see. But there she was. A young woman maybe eighteen, hiding under the floorboards. Her body so skinny and covered in filth she was barely recognizable. Her eyes were outlined in black and her face bore the scars of a blade. Her hair had been shaved from her head but had started to grow back in clumps.

I knew immediately that this was the hidden girl Sarah that Joshua had given his life to protect and written about before he was caught.

She looked as if she was trying to scream. Tears ran down her face. I saw Levitt looking down and shaking his head in disbelief. This was the first of these human tragedies that we had seen alive in days. We had become immune to cruelty and death, but maybe not to the fate worse.

Survival.

Timmons reached out his hand and a low, growing shriek came from the girl, like a trapped animal.

He took off his jacket and wrapped it gently around her. She was too weak to fight back. He then slowly pulled her from under the floor cradling her over his arms and resting her gently on the floor beside the three of us. For a moment he looked back at me, his eyes swollen with tears he tried to deny.

"Mills" Timmons spoke "Give me your water" I regained composure upon the suggestion.

Suddenly the coarse darkness that had built a shell of cynicism and despair around us for weeks was cracked open and the light of hope began to shine within us again.

I grabbed my canteen and while Timmons held her head up I poured it slowly over her face, washing it with my hands. Levitt's voice was slowly mumbling something gentle in a language I could not understand.

The girl trembled at the touch of the water. As I wiped her face Levitt broke into tears and laughter at the same time.

Timmons stood up and walked towards the door and lit a cigarette, staring out at the camp as if seeing it for the first time. He dropped to one knee and sobbed.

Since finding Sarah, the three of have taken eight-hour shifts guarding her and feeding her. We do not want others to know about her yet. She would be handed over to the medics and taken to an infirmary somewhere in Europe. She is too weak and scared.

We brought in blankets for her since she would not move from the spot. Levitt often sings to her in Polish. His voice is gentle and it seems to bring her calmness.

Timmons sits with her silently mostly; ever vigilant that she has water and food.

-HOWARD

May 12, 1945

After a few days in which it looked like she would not make it, Sarah has started to gain enough strength to sit up. She seems to trust us, mostly Timmons. Even during Levitt and my shifts, he stays close by as if he cannot leave her. It is as if he has been transformed from a man completely comfortable with death to a man clinging to the hope for life through her.

I have a plan today to have Levitt ask Sarah if she remembers Joshua, this kind man who is immortalized in this book, or Nigel, the wise yet mad man from the beginning. I do not know if she can yet speak. Maybe if he writes it down she will understand.

I need to know more about Joshua. I need to understand his kindness and somehow find a way to bring it to light for anyone associated with him. Sarah may be his last link to his life. Without her or this journal, he may be lost forever.

I will stop writing now, as I must get some rest.

I will write again tomorrow, God willing.

-HOWARD

May 1945—A few days since my last entry

Last night something happened that I must document.

Sarah awoke at about three thirty in the morning, screaming in German as she had other nights. I ran in to find Timmons waking up near her. He would not leave her side. Levitt came around the corner shortly after. As the three of us had become accustomed to, we gave her water and tried to calm her down

We had a room with a small cot setup just next to the space where we had found her. We were never far away. Sarah trusted me. She trusted Timmons as well. Levitt was harder on her but they were connected through their common ancestry and language. Somehow her survival was difficult for him to stomach. She was a reminder of what had happened to those of his heritage, and I think it provoked a fear and an anger that he did not want to feel.

He was colder to her than Timmons or I, often scolding at her as she screamed.

Despite his demeanor, I knew he cared and I often would catch him singing to her as she slept, the same Polish song he had sung the night we found her.

Tonight Sarah spoke for the first time. Levitt translated for her.

"Where am I?" she uttered. Levitt moved to her "Safe. You are Safe. We are Americans," he said softly.

She looked at me and then looked away. "Where is he?" she then said, looking towards the window. Her eyes were glassy but she was alert.

"Where is who Sarah?" Levitt asked. I moved closer to her.

"Water." she said, this time in English and smiling slightly. She motioned as if raising a cup to her lips.

"Mills? You want to see Mills?" Levitt assumed she remembered me from the day we found her as I had offered her my canteen. He motioned to me with his left hand and I started towards her.

I was so excited. Somehow she had awakened. Some of her humanity was creeping back into her ravaged mind. Maybe it was Levitt and the songs he had sung to her. Maybe it was the stoicism of Timmons or my nervous attention to her. Somehow we had broken through.

I lowered myself to one knee and she slightly raised her head.

I heard her slowly whisper it to me.

"Joshua."

-JOSH
Today is September 1, 2001

The drive home today was silent and uncomfortable at best. There is nothing comfortable about putting to rest someone like my father.

My name is Josh Mills. I am the son of Howard and Sarah Mills.

As you can tell if you have read this far, my parents named me after a kind stranger who apparently saved my Mother from a Nazi death camp during the war.

I knew my mother had been in a camp. She bore the numbers on her arm. But I never knew her story. I never knew of the man for whom I was named. I found this book, a diary of sorts, in the attic of my parents' home after my father passed away five days ago.

My father never talked of the War. I knew he had met my mother in Europe while deployed, but I never knew the circumstances. To read this account and to understand the sacrifices and the care he had shown her, rescuing her from the ruins of the Nazi camp and then devoting the next half-century of his life to her and her memory.

I wondered what had happened to Timmons and Levitt after the war; these great and kind men, so very different but bound by the inhumanity they witnessed and the glimmer of hope my mother had given them.

I wondered if my father had ever found Joshua's family, or if any had survived.

My father was buried today and I feel a great loss. He was sick mostly from a heart broken when he lost his best friend and his reason for life for some forty-five years.

We lost mother back in 1991. She fought long and hard, and I saw my father shrink from sadness and despair for the next ten years. He would sometimes sit next to the bed just staring for hours and hours. Only now do I understand that to him, she was still there. Since finding her in the camp, he lived his life to make her comfortable and safe.

In many ways, they saved each other.

Mother was wise and strong. She hardly resembled the shell of a woman I read about on the previous pages and it is difficult for me to place her there. But she adored my father, and now I know a little more why.

I don't know if my father ever found Joshua's family as he set out to. The diary ends as abruptly and mysteriously as it starts. It seems that my father simply stopped writing once he and my mother started to communicate.

The notion that this book has been passed between the fingers of four separate men, now including mine, makes me feel I must continue to write. It seems my duty.

The first few chapters are so bizarre, making me wonder if Nigel himself wrote them in madness in his final days in the death camp. If there really was a Nigel, how could he have imagined things so creative and unlike anything I had ever read or believed.

I may never know all of the facts, but I somehow understand that my existence was brought about by a chain of events that may not have happened without the sacrifice of this man called Joshua, and the kindness of my father, Private Howard Mills and his two fellow soldiers Stan Levitt and George Timmons.

My first order of action is to look for Levitt and Timmons to see if they are alive. I must show them how it all worked out for my father and for Sarah, the girl they had so lovingly brought back to life so many lifetimes ago.

I yearn to thank them, not only for my Mother's life, but for my own. It has become abundantly clear that I may have never existed if not for the kindness and sacrifice of these men.

I will write more tomorrow. Tonight, I just want to remember Dad.

-JOSH

September 9, 2001

I haven't written for a few days. I have spent much of my time preoccupied with thoughts of the contents of this journal, which with each reading brings forth new and unusual emotions. Some of it is very hard to read, such as the treatment of my mother and the others at the camp. Some if it is beautiful, such as Nigel's descriptions of the afterlife.

Joshua's message of service inspires me. I feel a burning need to know more.

It is September 9th today and I have an appointment to meet a Mrs. Genevieve Timmons, wife and widow of the late George Timmons, a friend of my fathers. I have not told anyone about the journal, just you who is reading this.

If you are reading this, I do not know what year it is in your time or how you have come to possess this book. Maybe, like me, you found it tucked away somewhere, hidden with the secrets of your past.

For me, it has unlocked an anxious and morbid curiosity to find out more about my Mother's time in captivity, and the mysterious Joshua, who risked his life daily for the others in the camp and somehow ensured my existence with his kindness.

Part of me wonders if there is a natural origin of the first few chapters. They are almost like a fantasy, taking place in a different world or dimension. You, of course, have already read that far and may understand my zealous craving for more knowledge.

It seems to me that I must work backwards starting with my own heritage. I must begin with Howard Mills and the mysterious girl under the floor called Sarah, who would become my mother. I must trace father's writings back, starting with his colleagues, those two unselfish men, Timmons and Levitt.

In all of my fifty-four years father never mentioned either of them. Nor mother. It was as if they had vanished forever. I often think that the evil that they witnessed changed them. I fantasize that they had to completely transform, absolving themselves of their memories, to be free of the cruelty they had witnessed. If not, they could risk becoming forever immune to human suffering.

It's relatively hard to think about my parents with a past so dark, but still more difficult to think of the things that my mother must have endured. I now consider and truly appreciate the strength of my father for the years he spent with her, never leaving her side until her final breath of life on this plane of existence.

If there is a Service Plane as Nigel describes in the first few pages, I know my father has found it. It gives me comfort, as unexplainable as it is compelling.

I am not a deeply religious man. My father was an Irish Catholic and my mother quite obviously Jewish by heritage. We were raised a bit different than other children. Rather than clinging to a denomination or even a static identity of an almighty being, we were taught the diversity and history of the various religions. We would celebrate Easter, but also Passover. Dad once took me to a Mosque and we sat silently as the prayers took place.

My father used to tell me that all religions were of the same basic principle. Love in the form of Service.

I must make my drive to New York now. Mrs. Timmons lives in Long Island. I can't wait to meet her, to somehow thank her and to honor the memory of her husband for my existence.

-JOSH

September 10—Later in the evening

My meeting with Mrs. Timmons was even more remarkable than I had anticipated.

It turns out that the late Sergeant George Timmons, then Private Timmons, had met his future wife, Genevieve Brouchelet, in Normandy a few days after the D-Day invasion. She told me how George stumbled to her farmhouse, wounded and scared. He had been separated from his unit and was lost, wandering the country alone. He had been hiding for days.

She spoke perfect English to me but told me that at the time, in 1944, she understood none and Timmons didn't speak a word of French. Her parents had fled Normandy when the Germans occupied, but she, despite their protests, had refused to leave.

She moved towards the oak mantle that rested above what was once a fireplace and was now sealed. Her fingers glossed across pictures scattered over her mantle and she pulled one down.

"This was George with your father and Stan." she said as she smiled slightly.

I looked at the black and white photo. It looked as if it could have been taken at camp. There was barbed wire fencing in the background and what looked to be barracks. The three men looked like children dressed as soldiers.

I looked up at her, my eyes giving away my next question.

"Yes. That was at the Nazi camp where they found the Jewish people." She paused and her thoughts seemed to fade.

"Your mother." she said without any prompt from me. Her eyes looked more solemn now.

"George left something of himself in that camp, or maybe brought something of the camp home." she sighed with a contrived smile.

"Mrs. Timmons" I started as I looked into her eyes, trying to bring her back into the moment. "Your husband helped to save my Mother's life in that camp." I stumbled for words.

Her eyes lowered back to the photo. "I knew your father," she said, "…and your mother."

She sat back down and continued.

"George swore he would come back to Normandy for me, and he did. But he was not alone. With him was a young girl, maybe eighteen at the time. She looked very sick, very bad. For nearly two months the three of us stayed at my family farm.

Then one day, your father showed up. I'll never forget him. He looked like Marlon Brando only taller. His eyes were so sincere and he was charming. He was not a quiet man like George at all. Very outgoing" She looked lost, her age clearly slowing down her thoughts and manner of expression.

"Are you Ok Mrs. Timmons?" I inquired.

"Oh Yes. I just haven't thought of your father for a very long time, or your mother." She sat on the couch and held the picture tightly.

"George and your father both seemed so worried about Sarah. She spoke very little and seemed afraid all of the time. It was hard for me to understand, but I knew that the Germans had done awful things to her."

She shook her head in disapproval and continued.

"But one night, she woke up screaming and I ran to her side. I passed through the hallway and I saw your father heading towards her room. When we reached the door, it was open and we heard crying. George was holding your mother, whispering softly to her, sobbing with her.

She looked up at Howard and the crying stopped. George stood up, cradling her like an infant in his outstretched arms and gently passed her to your father.

That very next day your father left with Sarah and brought her here to the United States where they were married within a year. They were so young, but we all were back then."

She paused and stared at the ground as she spoke. "We saw them once after that, at Stan Levitt's funeral" Her tone trailed off.

"Levitt, What ever happened to him?" I asked, later wishing I hadn't.

"When Stan came back from the war he rented a room in Long Island about three miles from us. George had found a job working on the telephone systems after he brought me to America and it placed us right here in this house."

She stopped and surveyed the room as if it was new to her, then continued.

"For the next two years George would get late night phone calls. Stan was always drunk, always in trouble. He was like a younger brother to George. He would get up in the middle of the night and go get Stan out of jail or wherever he was. He would bring him home to our sofa to sleep it off." She slightly touched her index finger over the picture of Stan Levitt as if massaging his face.

"He was a good man, Stan." Her voice quivered slightly.

"Then one day, I came home from the market and found him on the couch. He didn't move. He looked so peaceful. I saw his hand extended on the floor holding the gun. I knew what had happened. I didn't need to see the blood."

Sensing that this was too much for her, I took her hand and slowly pried the picture away, placing her teacup in its place.

Stan Levitt had committed suicide in George Timmons Long Island residence in 1951. I can only surmise and partially understand that what he had seen and experienced simply proved too much, and he lost all hope.

"One last question Mrs. Timmons" I pleaded softly. She looked up and smiled, her eyes swollen with tears. "Did George ever mention the name Joshua from the camp?" "Joshua?" She paused.

"No. He always told me the only survivor's name he knew from the camp was Sarah. He said it was all he wanted to know."

There was nothing else said that night. I left the Timmons home at about 6:30pm and my drive back was long and reflective.

I thought about my father finding the broken girl who would become my mother hiding in the death camp barely alive.

I thought of Joshua, the man who had saved my mother's life by hiding her and bringing her food and water. How can I thank him? How can I be of service as he was? What if he had valued his own life over hers? What if he had never read the words in this book and lived out Love in the form of Service?

I have business in New York City at the Trade Center tomorrow.

I will write more when I return.

-JOSH

September 11, 2001 8:00am

My conversation with Mrs. Timmons, while moving, was a dead end for locating Joshua. As a result, I have turned my focus to work. Maybe it has to be enough to know that the humanity of a man like Joshua existed in such a time. Yet the bothersome thing is that all those who he helped, my mother and the countless others that he may have hidden and brought water to and eventually gave his life for, are all gone.

If not for this strange journal, the one in which I continue to write, there would be nothing left of him.

I wonder if there are others like me who exist today because of the kindness of those who preceded them. This whole idea of fate and the strange and disjointed contents of Nigel's early diary and Joshua's application of it have provoked thoughts in me of fatalism and the true nature of faith and even human existence that I am not sure I will ever be able to separate from my consciousness.

For today though I will focus on my real work. At my age I still enjoy what I do, but I'm often tired of doing it. I have not yet written about this but I have two children, Thomas and Bridget. My wife Deidra and I met in Dublin while I was a young man working abroad. We have been married nearly twenty-five years now.

Thomas is away at school on the west coast and Bridget graduated last spring and works in Chicago as a paralegal. She plans to go back to law school after a few years.

Growing up with my father, he never mentioned the liberation of the camp or how he and my mother came to be together. He never mentioned Timmons or Levitt and until I read this journal and his brief account of those days in 1945, I had no idea. I knew he was in World War II and I knew my mother was a prisoner at some point. They had both just told me that they had met during the War.

When I think of this I realize the circumstances of the fate of my own children. Had I not taken a business trip to Dublin in 1971 I would have never met my future wife, and of course, not produced my future children. This concept seems understandable and the faith that I derive from it seems almost natural. But the thought that my parents met under the blanket of such darkness and evil and that in order for my mother to live many had to die is an insurmountable climb of spiritual belief to me. I cannot accept the facts written earlier in this text; that evil drives all that is good and that the Balance of good requires the influx of evil. I want to live in a world that is good. I want to be given hope for humanity and the statements I've read and the events surrounding my very own existence strike nothing but a cold and stark realism that translates to an existential fear of my own fate.

Does this make me selfish, or unwilling to serve? I ask myself these questions as I write this morning. I will continue to write tomorrow.

For now it is off to the Trade Center and a little work.

-JOSH

September 11, 2001
11:50AM

I know at this moment that this will be my last entry in this book. I know now what Joshua felt when his death was drawing near.

I will recount what has happened as best I can. I do not know if this will ever be read. It may very well be engulfed in the flames that surround me.

Some people here have said that this was an act of war against the United States. I do not know. From my office high in Tower One, I watch fighter jets scramble the city. Some of those trapped with me have chosen to jump from the windows, I will not.

I want my children to know I did not jump. In fact, I want them to know that my destiny, the summit of every event of my life, has led me to this place today, and for a reason; to realize my true purpose and to maybe save the lives of

109

others. I have been placed here for reasons I may never know.

I have no phone to call my dear wife. She will find out I have passed later today.

After the initial explosion we tried to get to the exit but the flames blocked the door. The floor below us seemed uneasy from the beginning. It shook and wavered and the smoke and flames continued to climb.

There are many of us here on the south side. Some are familiar and some I do not recognize.

We know that the only chance we have is to stifle the flames long enough to get the fire door opened and then run as fast as we can to the stairwell. Once there we have a chance.

They have a chance.

A few moments ago a young man, maybe in his early thirties with a slight accent, slid on the floor next to me. He spoke with a familiar voice although I don't know where from, and that is as much as I can say about him.

He said to me, "My friend, there are a dozen people here who will live and I may not be one of them." I looked at him startled.

"No. We will all get out of here," I said, choking back smoke. He grabbed me by one shoulder and looked me dead in the eye. "Listen man, I have nothing to do for this moment but help these people get down that stairwell so they can go live their lives, have their babies, and serve their Maker as I have served mine"

My face dropped. I knew exactly what he meant. It was as if he lifted the words from the lips of Joshua and Nigel and my Father; of those who wrote in the journal before me.

I thought of Joshua and his selfless acts to save the prisoners including my mother. I also know now what I must do and why I am here in this burning building.

You see, it will take two of us to save the others, one to hold the door while the other tries to subdue the flames with the extinguisher. This will give them a few seconds, just enough time for them to get to the stairwell. From there, fate will carry them back into the world to live and serve.

I know this is the way.

If my family is reading this someday, I do not want you to mourn me, but rather feel peace and joy. Know that I ended my time here in Service and that I found the way to repay Joshua, Levitt, Timmons and my parents for their sacrifice and courage.

This moment was always meant to be, and I was always meant to do this. It is always that way.

To my children, always realize that you are the product of a chain of human kindness and self-sacrifice that should never be forgotten. Live in service to others as payment to those who have passed from the Living Plane to ensure your existence.

To anyone else who reads this, take in the pages of this book fully and do not hate those who committed this act. Do not live in a prison of resentment and hatred.

I must now pass this book to someone who will live to carry this message.

My Entry is approaching.

I feel peace.

Your husband, your father and your friend . . .

-Josh

-DORIS

September 11, 2011

It has been ten years since that day on which my life was saved.

Josh, one of the men who saved me, gave me this book and asked me not to open it until I could give back what he had given me.

I have gone through so much change since then, emotionally, spiritually and now even physically.

For the first few years I was so angry and so afraid. I mourned for those lost and hated those who did this to us, because I didn't understand. I still do not, but today I feel a sense of peace knowing I am not supposed to understand.

First you must know more about how I came to have this book. I remember so vividly what happened.

I was a secretary at a financial firm, just in my twenties at the time. I worked on one of the upper floors of Tower

One. We knew we had been attacked but not how. I didn't know about the planes until days later.

Ever since the early nineties when a bombing attempt was made on the Trade Center, routine reminders were in place for just such an event. We knew the Towers were a target but we lived in complacency, going about our lives as if tomorrow was somehow guaranteed.

Flames and smoke filled the floor where we were. The fires were scattered in small islands. Papers floated through the air like wounded butterflies. There was a chemical smell to the fire. Jet fuel maybe, as I later learned.

We huddled together in groups, paralyzed by fear. Some cried and some prayed. We were in an incomprehensible state of panic and chaos.

But the two men were like angels.

As the flames closed in on us, I heard a man with an Irish sounding accent stand up and pronounce; "Ladies and Gentlemen, it is time for us to get the hell out of here" He was smiling while he talked.

A warm calm came over me, like the one I feel today.

Then I saw Josh standing just behind him. He reminded me of my own father and the minute I saw him I knew he was a special man.

The man with the accent asked us to assemble about ten feet from the door. The flames on the other side of the door were crackling like a huge fireplace. I was terrified.

Josh and the man took three desks and placed them in front of us to block the blaze. They asked us to lie down on the floor behind the desks. They didn't lie down though. Josh stood on top of one of the desks holding the extinguisher and the younger stood next to him.

As I looked up through the smoke I saw the Irish sounding man whisper something into Josh's ear. Josh looked him directly in the eye and nodded.

Suddenly the man spoke again "I am going to count to three and this door will come open. I would then ask you to hold your breath, close your eyes and run as fast as you can to the stairwell. Once there, head down and do not stop. You will feel the cold foam from the extinguisher, and the smoke will burn your eyes, but you must not stop, no matter what."

We looked at each other terrified. Some cried and some prayed. There were about twelve of us in the group, maybe more.

The man with the accent spoke again, "One more thing ladies and gentlemen. This brave lad behind me, Mr. Josh Mills, will provide cover with the extinguisher. You must move quick if he is to have a chance to save you."

He paused and looked at Josh. "We will be right behind you."

I knew they wouldn't.

There were more cries, some screams. We knew what was about to happen.

He bent his knees as if to jump down from the desk but then rose back up as his voice became slightly louder.

"...And one last thing friends" He smiled and exhaled "May God be with each of you." It was the most comforting smile I have ever seen.

At this point I knew there was a very small chance that I was going to live. I knew that this was a crazy, last ditch effort and if I walked through that door I could be burned alive or I could fall to my death. I then thought of these two men who would surely have no chance if they provided our escape route.

I stood up and walked towards them.

When I reached them I grabbed the man with the accent by the collar of his shirt and pulled him towards me sobbing hysterically. "You will be killed! He will be killed!" I struggled to get the words out.

To this day have never spoken of what happened, but I swear with every fiber in my soul that this is true.

He leaned to me and whispered in my ear.

"Doris my sister today is not your day to Enter. For me and for Josh, it is time. You will live and when you can be of Service, you will."

I was stunned. How did he know my name? But I knew he was right. I could feel it. It was an insane sort of faith that I had never felt before. I found a strange sense of contentment in the implausibility that this man knew my fate, and I believed him.

Josh the approached me. He reached into his jacket and handed me a book. This book. It was weathered and tattered. I had no idea until yesterday what it contained. As he handed it to me he asked me "What is your name".

"Doris" I told him.

"Doris. You must be brave and help these people to get out. You will be their guide. You will lead them through the smoke and to their safety. Get them home. You will be brave."

He spoke as if giving me orders, but in a kind tone.

"I would also like to ask you to find my wife and children and to tell them that I will always love them, and that I will see them again."

His eyes welled with tears as he spoke.

He then took the wrist of my hand that contained the book and shook it gently.

"Open this in ten years to this day. You will know what to do."

Josh Mills looked directly into my eyes as he spoke and I felt a warmth and love that I have never felt before or since.

I looked over his shoulder and saw the man with the accent nod at Josh. Josh raised the extinguisher braced himself atop the line of desks, flames crackling all around him.

The rest is a blur. A door opened, we all ran and here I am today, telling you all about it.

I've spent ten years wondering why they died and why I lived.

The nurses are coming now. I will write more tomorrow.

-DORIS

September 13, 2011

I have not written in a few days. I must tell you that my health is very bad. I am confined to this bed in this hospital as my brain has been ravaged by disease. I often wonder why I was spared in the towers only to suffer this way.

However, the events of my life have been quite extraordinary by normal standards and I do believe now that this is just the beginning of my journey.

I have been reading this book and working backwards mostly while finding unbelievable coincidences in the pages. I know for a fact that Josh Mills was real. I was the last person still alive to see him. What is more bizarre and more puzzling is the Irish sounding man who stood with Josh, and who offered such reassurance to us as he faced certain death. I will write more about that later.

Every one of us except for those two got out alive that day. I have lived my life since then honoring their memory. I have told parts of their story and have honored Josh's last request to me.

I have come to know and love Josh's wife and children as my own family. They visit me in the hospital each week.

Of the man with the accent, this angel who provided comfort and calm and accepted his own fate willingly and almost joyfully, I knew nothing. But today, as I read to the beginning of the book as Josh asked me to a decade ago, I realize that there is one last tribute I must pay.

It must be paid to ensure the Balance.

I have been tested to find out which organs are still healthy. I am told that all but my brain are unaffected by the tumor. Disease chooses its own place in the body. It's cold and calculated and hardly random. The sickness has its own agenda and its own soul. But it is not evil.

Nothing really is.

I realize as I read further into the writings of Nigel that this is a mobilization of the Takers on my behalf. I am being called to Service, but not without one final test, one that it is impossible for me to fail.

I feel the presence of a great love and peace around me even in my times of tremendous pain. I sometimes feel like Josh and the accented man are still here as they were in the Towers all those years ago; Josh reassuring me with his crooked smile that I will end up exactly where I am supposed to be.

The sedatives are starting to take effect. I feel calm and tired. I will write more soon.

I sense the Gatherers. They are coming.

-DORIS

September 15, 2011

Something astounding has occurred today. I must share it with you.

As I continued to read, I came to realize who the man with the accent was, and why he was in that building with me. I realize that there are no coincidences and that human existence is purely a phase of destiny that each of us must pass through to earn our next assignment, and find our measure of usefulness to maintain the Balance and serve the Maker.

As I write this I feel unexplainable tranquility.

Bridget and Thomas, Josh's children, are here with me. They have become my family. I feel his presence and I know I must continue to write as long as I can. Eventually the disease will take my memories and my ability to share this, so I must write it down today. With each passing day I feel myself slipping away from the Living Plane. I know that soon I will simply stop existing here. I have asked them not to put me on life support, as I know my Service is needed somewhere else. They have given me mere weeks.

So I must write.

I must tell you how I know what my purpose is. This is the part that to you will seem unbelievable, yet after reading this you will see that life is an endless circle. There is no time and there is no destination. Death is a beginning not an end and every action, every breath we take, decides the next task. We are in a constant, timeless state of Entry and Exit, each story leaving its imprint on the next or the previous.

I am thinking back to the Towers now. Flames were everywhere. The heat was unbearable, but I knew that I would live. I knew these two men would save me.

After confronting the man with the accent I released him and sobbed. I knew that he would die that day and I knew that I would live on.

This is the part that I did not remember until today, until I read this book passed to me by Josh Mills.

I turned to the gentleman and I asked him his name.

He whispered in my ear.

"Galen" he said. "My name is Galen".

Josh Mills along with Galen saved my life and the lives of twelve others that day.

Galen, the Advocate who inspired the early chapters of this book was there. It was his day of Entry.

I understand. Today I know how Nigel became Joshua and that he had to bring Howard with him so he could save Sarah. Howard and Sarah created Josh and Josh saved my life and the lives of others. Galen was there with him, guiding him through his Entry. I am just a channel through which a spirit passes. I am the spirit of all of them. I am the spirit of the Maker.

So today I serve the Maker the only way I know how and I ensure the Balance.

I write and I carry their message of Service through my actions.

I have read through this book I believe that all of us are part of the Balance. Our combined Energy ensures each of our existence. Our fates are intertwined, each depending on the fate of those before or after us.

I remember what Nigel wrote

"No one of us has the Energy to return alone, so we must travel with companions. Our combined Energy, the Energy of all of us, allows us to exist in the spiritual dimension and to maintain the Balance as the Maker wants."

A doctor visited me from Chicago today and he gave me my answer. He told me why I was saved in the Towers, why I am dying and why I came to have this book.

There was a list of names of people whom I could help. One name stood out. It is a young boy.

I must go now. I can no longer write today. But I now know who I am writing to. I am writing to you.

You are part of this story. Somewhere in time, maybe past or maybe future, you have ensured the Balance.

Someday we will meet, or maybe we already have.

-DORIS
December 18, 2011

I am Doris Murphy. This is my final entry.

I wrote this while I was still healthy enough to write, and asked Thomas Mills, son of Josh Mills, to enter the date above it upon my Entry. I then gave him very explicit instructions on where to send this book.

I was diagnosed with an inoperable brain tumor. I did not know the reason until your name was given to me.

Today I have passed away quietly in my sleep surrounded by loved ones and family. I have accepted this choice as it has been made for me.

My healthy organs will be removed from this vessel and one will be placed into the body of a young man, and he will enjoy health and happiness in his time here and someday we will meet when it is his time to return to the Service Plane.

It will begin with him and it will never end. Time and space will have no meaning in our existence. Each of our roles will feed the Balance and each of us will ensure that life continues.

As a result of all of the events in this journal, you will live to feel both joy and pain. You will lead a useful life, and struggle through its lessons, until the time when you are called to the Service Plane.

Someday I know you will honor my love in the form of service as so many have honored yours.

By the time you read this, you will understand. It doesn't matter what your name is, or what the date of your existence is, you are somehow part of our story. All of us are one. Look beyond the things you understand. Know that the Maker is all that is, and that his power drives all things peaceful, painful, joyful and real.

If you look back on the circumstances surrounding your life you will find that someone or something provided a means for you to exist. A few mere twists of fate and you never exist, nor your family and all those whom you have touched. Your very existence is the product of a chain of timeless events, past and present, which cannot be explained but had to happen in the exact order and manner in which they did. The good and the bad had to happen for you to be one with us.

Maybe it was a close call that didn't kill you, a mistake that was forgiven, a turning point in your life that you cannot explain or a time of tragedy that eventually gave way to peace. There was someone or something there to help you find your way, your strength and your Energy.

Each person that you have helped through your compassion has ensured the Balance, and you have served the Maker. You have pleased Him.

These are not coincidences or products of human will. They are all your part in the Balance and we are all there to help you as you have always helped us. This is your truth. You are one with us.

Know peace today and we will meet, either in your past or in your future.

Doris14262

-Nigel

December 24, 2043

This journal was removed from the belongings of Ms. Doris Murphy, 38, of Hoboken NJ at the time of her death in 2011.

Notably, Ms. Murphy was a survivor of the September 11, 2001 World Trade Center bombings.

The book arrived to my home via courier a few days ago. There was no return address. I do not know who sent it.

I have read it and realized that while Doris suffered at the end of life, she loved and served as needed.

The preceding pages were the final passage in her journal. Her words, and those which served as a prologue to her life, are the remarkable story of the very people who made my life possible.

I have felt compelled to document this chapter in her story, as it does not end in death. There is no end for any of us.

We do not evaporate and our Energy, love and courage live on.

Quite simply, as an organ donor, Ms. Murphy's healthy kidneys were removed and one transplanted into a very sick young man just twelve years old at the time.

As I have read this journal I have come to understand.

I have enjoyed exactly 14970 days on the Living Plane since that day thanks to Doris. Her final act was choosing my name from the list of those awaiting transplants. This saved my life.

As a result, I have served here and now I go to my next assignment.

As a doctor, I have spent my life on a mission to combat death and disease and have felt called to do so as if it were my sole purpose. My Father, John, died at a young age of a disease called Cancer leaving my mother to care for our family. In my father's last days he ensured that we would have everything we needed. He spent his final breaths providing for us, acting out of service. He was scared and angry, but he showed nothing but love and kindness. He was my teacher.

I myself was later found to have a rare kidney disorder and through the kindness of Doris Murphy, was allowed to live much longer than I should have.

I committed myself, through education and research, to ending the suffering that claimed my father and Doris.

My work has been my life, and my life has been relatively short, but I have served and I now must Enter.

I have lived and served here on Earth because of Doris. In the end, she found a way to serve the Balance. Yet, she lived because of Josh, who existed because of Howard and Sarah, who was saved by Joshua.

Joshua was a name given to Nigel when he Exited the Service Plane. It has come full circle and it makes sense.

I think of Doris' words.

"Death is a beginning, not an end and every action, every breath we take, decides the next action. We are in a constant, timeless state of Entry and Exit; each story leaving its imprint on the next or the previous." It was always to be.

I feel peace.

My name is Nigel15322.

I will never forget the day I died.

It was today.

-FINAL ENTRY

Dr. Nigel Stakes passed away today at his home of yet unknown causes.

Dr. Stakes is credited with groundbreaking research that isolated the genetic makeup of the centuries old epidemic known as Cancer.

Cancer, which is documented to have claimed hundreds of millions of human lives, was completely eradicated due to Dr. Stakes work.